Acclaim

"*Money Shot* is a stunner, careening along with a wild, propulsive energy and a deliciously incendiary spirit. Laced with bravado and loaded up with knockabout charm, Christa Faust's Hard Case debut is the literary equivalent of a gasoline cocktail."

—*Megan Abbott*

"An instant pulp classic."

—*Rolling Stone*

"I was sucked into the tight, juicy *Money Shot*, from the ripping car trunk start to the hard-pumping climax. This novel is so convincing that you want to believe Faust has been an oversexed, naked killing machine, at least once."

—*Vicki Hendricks*

"*Money Shot* is smart, stylish, insightful, fast-paced pulp fiction with razor-sharp humor and a kick-ass heroine. Christa Faust is a super crime writer."

—*Jason Starr*

"*Money Shot* makes most crime novels seem about as exciting as the missionary position on a Tuesday night. The results are stunning."

—*Duane Swierczynski*

"Wonderfully lurid, with attitude to spare and a genuine affection for the best of hardboiled traditions. Christa Faust is THE business."

—*Maxim Jakubowski*

"Christa Faust writes like she means it. *Money Shot* is dark, tough, stylish, full of invention and builds to one hell of a climax."
—*Allan Guthrie*

"Christa Faust proves she can run with the big boys with this gritty thriller set in the darkest places of the porn industry. I loved it!"
—*McKenna Jordan, Murder By the Book*

"Never has an avenging Angel been sexier. *Money Shot* leaves you spent and wanting more."
—*Louis Boxer, founder of NoirCon*

"Entertaining and all that neo-pulp should be, but its ring of authenticity also makes it quite a bit more than that."
—*Sarah Weinman*

"The story had me from the first pages."
—*Bill Crider*

"Christa Faust's first Angel Dare mystery, *Money Shot*, caused a sensation...Faust rewrote the femme fatale guidebook and upended the whole noir spectrum."
—*L.A. Review of Books*

"Christa Faust's *Money Shot* has to be an early contender for mystery debut of the year...*Money Shot* has no peer."
—*Bloomberg News*

"Angel Dare," he said. "As I live and breathe."

For a second, we both just stood there. Wind whipped my damaged, coppery hair into my face, but his hat stayed on like it was nailed on. I was trying to make my lips move, to formulate some kind of denial, anything at all, but my thoughts were a scattered jumble, and nothing came out.

He smiled and reached into an inner pocket, and I figured he's gonna shoot me right here in this shitty gas station and hey, at least I won't have to worry about the Situation anymore.

He didn't shoot me. He pulled out a badge. A fucking cop, but that made me feel worse, not better.

His smile grew, wide and cruel. I was pretty sure his perfect teeth were fake.

"I love your movies," he said, tucking the badge back into the pocket it came from.

So, it was like that. Fine. Nothing I couldn't handle...

HARD CASE CRIME BOOKS BY CHRISTA FAUST:

MONEY SHOT
CHOKE HOLD
THE GET OFF
PEEPLAND (*graphic novel, with Gary Phillips*)

SOME OTHER HARD CASE CRIME BOOKS YOU WILL ENJOY:

JOYLAND *by Stephen King*
THE COCKTAIL WAITRESS *by James M. Cain*
THIEVES FALL OUT *by Gore Vidal*
SO NUDE, SO DEAD *by Ed McBain*
QUARRY *by Max Allan Collins*
THE KNIFE SLIPPED *by Erle Stanley Gardner*
SNATCH *by Gregory Mcdonald*
THE LAST STAND *by Mickey Spillane*
UNDERSTUDY FOR DEATH *by Charles Willeford*
THE TRIUMPH OF THE SPIDER MONKEY *by Joyce Carol Oates*
BLOOD SUGAR *by Daniel Kraus*
LEMONS NEVER LIE *by Donald E. Westlake writing as Richard Stark*
ARE SNAKES NECESSARY? *by Brian De Palma and Susan Lehman*
KILLER, COME BACK TO ME *by Ray Bradbury*
FIVE DECEMBERS *by James Kestrel*
THE NEXT TIME I DIE *by Jason Starr*
LOWDOWN ROAD *by Scott Von Doviak*
SEED ON THE WIND *by Rex Stout*
FAST CHARLIE *by Victor Gischler*
NOBODY'S ANGEL *by Jack Clark*
DEATH COMES TOO LATE *by Charles Ardai*
INTO THE NIGHT *by Cornell Woolrich and Lawrence Block*

The GET OFF

by **Christa Faust**

A HARD CASE CRIME BOOK
(HCC-166)
First Hard Case Crime edition: March 2025

Published by

Titan Books
A division of Titan Publishing Group Ltd
144 Southwark Street
London SE1 0UP

in collaboration with Winterfall LLC

Author Photo by David Suh

Print edition ISBN 978-1-83541-173-5
E-book ISBN 978-1-83541-174-2

Design direction by Max Phillips
www.signalfoundry.com

Typeset by Swordsmith Productions

Printed and bound by CPI (UK) Ltd, Croydon CR0 4YY

Visit us on the web at www.HardCaseCrime.com

For Pop Faust and The Alabama Slamma, Ross Hill.
Two men who caught the Westbound Train before they had a chance to read the book they inspired.

THE GET OFF

1.

They called me a femme fatale in the media, back when that Jesse Black fiasco went down. Most people have no idea what it really means. Most people think it means badass with tits, but that's not it at all. A real femme fatale is a villain, and I always thought of myself as a hero. At least I tried to be.

Turned out they were right.

May, 2011.

I found out I was pregnant on my way to kill Vukasin.

I'd been stalking him, online and in real life. I followed him everywhere, obsessively studying his daily habits. Letting him think he was hunting me, when I was really hunting him.

I started fucking his urologist about three weeks ago. Dr. Albert Balian was a sweet guy but utterly clueless when it came to women. Middle aged, unattractive, unhappily married. An easy mark. It was no sweat to convince him how hot it would be for me to dress up like one of his nurses and blow him under the desk in his cluttered office during business hours. At first, he'd been resistant to the idea of me wearing the boring unisex scrubs his real nurses wear and wanted me in some kind of skimpy stripper fantasy getup made out of red and white vinyl. I wore him down, claiming it would be so much sexier for me if I could imagine he was my real boss and that I might lose my job if I didn't do what he wanted. I'd done it just often enough for the rest of his long-suffering staff to get used to seeing me wearing scrubs around the office, but not enough for him to get bored with the whole idea.

When I stepped onto the elevator that day, I was locked and loaded. Pulse racing as I fought to slow my breathing and steady my hands. I had a capped syringe tucked into the pocket of my borrowed scrub pants, filled with enough potassium chloride to stop an elephant's heart. I was sweating under my expensive blonde wig. The tunnel vision of my aching hatred made me feel righteous and invincible. Nothing else mattered.

It was 2:20 PM as I stood alone in the elevator, waiting for the doors to close. Vukasin's appointment was for 2:30, so I still had time to get in through the back door and meet him in the one place his security goons didn't follow. He didn't want any of his men to see that hunk of badly reconstructed meat that dangled between his legs.

That's my fault, by the way. I didn't technically do it, but I was the catalyst that made it happen. If you just walked in on the middle of this low-budget action movie that my life has become, all you need to know for now is that he did shit to me and to people I love that I can't forgive. Not fucking ever. Hence, the mutual vendetta.

The doors on the elevator had started to slide closed when they suddenly bounced back open to admit a pregnant woman with a baby strapped into one of those carrier harnesses that make you look like you have a stunted and partially absorbed Siamese twin growing out of your chest.

The woman was flushed and cheerful with the same fluffy, strawberry blond hair as her equally pink-faced baby. She was dressed in roomy, colorful sweats and had a fancy designer diaper bag slung over one shoulder. The baby was wailing and hiccupping in ascending scales like a soprano warming up for a difficult aria.

"Whoo," the woman said, panting and leaning heavily against the left side of the elevator as she pressed the same glowing button that I had obviously already pressed. "Can't move so quick anymore."

I didn't answer. Just stared straight ahead at the closing doors.

"Is this your first?" she asked, lightly bouncing her fussing baby.

I turned to her with a baffled frown.

"This is my fourth," she said without waiting for my answer. The baby was starting to gasp and spit like it might blow a head gasket. "A little boy, finally, after three girls! I promise it gets so much easier after the first one. When are you due?"

The baby's high-pitched wailing was fraying my last nerve and making my fists curl and itch, but that woman's sweaty pink face was so mild and sweet, completely oblivious to the battle currently raging inside me. I was about to say something cruel to shut her the fuck up but didn't. I forced a smile that I hoped didn't seem too condescending.

"I'm not pregnant," I said, raising my voice to be heard over the crying baby and smoothing my scrubs over my admittedly bigger-than-I-might-have-liked belly. "I'm just fat."

She laughed and shook her head, like we were sharing some wonderful private joke. Her baby was still crying but starting to wind down as she continued with the bouncing and cooing.

"I know, right?" she said. "When my sister-in-law was pregnant with my nephew, she looked like an ad for prenatal yoga, all toned and glowing with this perfect round tummy. Me, I always look like I just escaped from Sea World."

She rooted around for a second in the outer pocket of the diaper bag, and I figured she was looking for some kind of pacifier or toy to help shut the baby up. Instead, she took out a small packet of tissues and held them out to me.

"They make pads," she said. "You should get some. At least while you're still working."

They make pads. That sentence was so far outside anything I expected from the conversation that for a moment I thought I misheard her.

"Pads?" I repeated, frown deepening.

Again, that light, happy laugh, like there was nothing wrong with the world. Like I wasn't about to go kill the man who had killed or helped kill pretty much everyone I ever cared about.

"Bra pads," she said, pressing the packet of tissues into my hand. "I didn't need them when I was pregnant with Olivia, my oldest. She had the hardest time latching and I ended up having to hire a lactation consultant just to get the taps running, but this time around I'm already a total colostrum fountain, just like you! Anyway, for now you can use these to absorb any excess and hopefully one of your coworkers will have a spare top they can lend you."

I looked down at my navy-blue scrub top. There were two small, damp blotches on the front, one over each nipple. I couldn't have been more horrified if I'd just realized I was covered in blood.

2.

The elevator doors opened, and the pregnant woman waddled off towards the OB/GYN down the hall from Dr. Balian, waving to me and saying something cheery and meaningless that I couldn't hear over the roaring inside my head.

I leaned against the wall of the elevator, feeling faint and sick and panicky. There had to be some other explanation for the blotches. Infection? Cancer? After all, I'm over 40 and always use condoms. I battled multiple bouts of pelvic inflammatory disease during my early years in the porn business and I had been told that I had reduced my chances of successful baby-making to somewhere between slim and none. I didn't care. I never wanted actual kid-kids anyway, and the girls I used to manage were all the daughters I ever needed.

I started scrolling back over every single recent sexual encounter since my last period. All with Dr. Balian and all with protection. Had there been a slip, an imperceptibly tiny rupture that could have allowed some wayward and ambitious sperm to breach the perimeter?

When was that latest spotty, half-assed period anyway? Was that two weeks ago? Three? Time had been collapsing in on itself as I fell deeper and deeper into my all-consuming stalker waltz with Vukasin.

The doors started to slide shut and I was forced to launch myself through before they closed on me. Standing in the long bland hallway, I took a moment to get my shit back together. I didn't have time for any of this. I was on a mission. So what if I was pregnant or dying from breast cancer or what fucking ever?

I could always go get an abortion or a mastectomy after Vukasin was dead. For now, I needed to stay calm, stay focused and do what needed to be done.

I headed down the hallway to the staff entrance of Dr. Balian's office.

I punched in the code to open the door. Mrs. Balian's birthday. So sweet. Once inside, I spotted a petite Armenian nurse, Ani I think her name was, coming down the hall in my direction with her eyes on a patient's chart. I quickly crossed my arms over my damp scrub top as she looked up and spotted me, not even bothering to try and hide her scathing disapproval.

I tried to see myself through her eyes for a moment, that trashy blonde slut with too much bronzer, electric blue contacts and fat red lips drawn way outside their natural shape. I wanted her to remember me that way, as a laundry list of exaggerated characteristics that she would later use to describe me to detectives, none of which have anything to do with the way I actually look. I smiled at her, and she turned away, ignoring me like I was a bad smell that she was too polite to acknowledge. She went into one of the exam rooms and closed the door while I ducked into the staff lounge.

The lounge was an odd little extra room with a stubby L shape. Table and chairs. Kitchenette. A cute little red couch, tucked into the short leg of the L. I blew Dr. Balian on that couch once, so I knew the door locked.

Once I locked it, I peeled off my damp scrub top. My sports bra was also stained but I knew I'd probably have to run after the deed was done and didn't want my possibly infected boobs flopping painfully up and down while I did it.

I took a quick peek under the spandex to see what was going on, nipplewise. They definitely seemed darker and stiffer than normal, sore to the touch. Was that new? How long had they been like that? The one on the left seemed a little crusty and when I prodded it with the tip of my finger, it oozed several tiny, pearlescent droplets. That had definitely never happened before. Another wave of dizzy, drowning anxiety threatened to close over my head.

I needed to pull myself together, to make myself breathe slow and clear my crazy head. I thought of a guy I used to know, of the way revenge can twist you up inside and make you forget who you'd always assumed you were. I had no idea who I was anymore or who I would be after this was over, but there was no time to worry about that now.

I folded two of the pregnant woman's tissues into squares, tucked them into my bra, and opened the closet door. Behind a few sad, forgotten jackets was a single spare scrub top. It was a bit tight over my tits and belly, but workable, and I tossed the stained one into the trash. My fingers reached for the capped syringe in my pants pocket like it was a rosary, but I was all out of prayers.

I checked my watch. Showtime.

3.

Vukasin wasn't in the first exam room. It was instead occupied by a tiny old man who beamed like he just won the lottery when I opened the door. He was visibly crestfallen when I told him I had the wrong room.

The next one was the right room.

When I saw Vukasin, I felt that hot surge of intense and complex emotion not unlike the way you feel when you spot your high school crush in the lunchroom. I'd been watching him for months through windows, binoculars, cameras or online, but this was the first time that we were actually in the same room together. First time since Vegas.

He'd been steadily losing weight that he couldn't spare. His angular face was haggard and unshaven, harshly lit from below by the glow of his phone. His thin white legs stuck out of the paper gown, knobby and restless like a child's. He seemed so small and defenseless, his body hunched and slightly embarrassed and just wanting to get this over with. Just a middle-aged guy at the doctor, like any other guy. Only he wasn't just any guy. He was *the one*, my anti-soulmate, as obsessed with killing me as I was with killing him. Our whole lives had been leading up to this intimate moment together.

"How are we today?" I asked, pitching my voice high and sweet like a preschool teacher as I slipped into a pair of nitrile gloves.

His eyes flicked up from the phone screen for a fraction of a second and I held my breath, sure that he would see right through my half-assed disguise. Like he would be able to smell me, to recognize me as his homicidal mate on some deep, primal level. But he dismissed me as irrelevant almost instantly, attention returning to his phone.

"Fine," he said, not because he was actually fine, but because that's just what you say when someone who doesn't matter asks how you are.

Emboldened by his thoughtless dismissal, I came forward and took his right wrist in my hand, pretending to check his pulse while I thumbed the cap off the syringe inside my pocket. He shifted the phone to his left hand and continued reading whatever it was he was reading. I could smell his breath, that sharp and horribly familiar scent of the peppermint gum he always chewed. Whenever I met someone else who chewed that same gum, the smell gave me this hot pulse of Pavlovian nausea. Ironic, since that particular brand is marketed primarily to lovers who want to taste good when they make out.

My hand was shaking when I raised it to place two fingers just below his right ear. I swallowed hard against the nausea and felt my vision narrow down to a dark, whirling tunnel centered around his carotid artery.

"Turn your head to the left, please," I said, hating the thin mousy squeak that had replaced my voice.

He did what I asked with a small, exasperated sigh, like I was a mildly annoying inconvenience. His eyes stayed glued to his phone.

This was it. Flipping the switch in my head and deciding to stop running and start hunting had been the only thing that kept me going. Everything I'd been through, the strange and lonely hell the last six months had been, it was all leading up to this. Nothing else mattered. I raised the syringe and held it poised a bare millimeter from that vein in his neck while I leaned in close to his ear.

"It's me," I said. "Angel."

Then I slid the needle into the vein. That's when the shooting started.

4.

I have this clear dividing line in my life, a bloody and traumatic Rubicon crossed the day of that ill-fated boy/girl shoot in Bel Air. A line between the life I used to have and what's happening now. What keeps on happening, this crazy minute-by-minute skin-of-my-teeth survival that in no way resembles any kind of life.

But the truth is more complicated, because it's not just one thing. It's a sliding scale, a series of transgressions. Things I never thought I could live through but somehow do anyway. Things that chip away at the polite illusion of who I once believed I was.

One of those things, a small piece of the big ugly mess, but yet huge and life changing on its own, is having been shot at. Also, having been hit. Once your body knows what that feels like, you never think maybe that sound is just firecrackers.

As I instinctively yanked Vukasin's body in front of mine, I realized several things at once. One was that my syringe was still sticking out of his neck, wobbling up and down with the plunger unplunged. Another was that it didn't matter anyway, because he had just been shot in the skinny, concave chest. Not dead yet but headed down that road at a decent clip and really fucking furious about it. Last and most significantly, the sudden appearance of the gun and the person behind it. Clearly, I wasn't the only one who thought this was a good place to take Vukasin out.

"Niko, you treacherous fucking bitch," Vukasin said, words muffled in my ringing ears and punctuated by a mist of blood around his cracked lips.

"Nothing personal," the shooter replied.

Niko. I recognized him instantly as one of Vukasin's accomplices from that horror show in Vegas. The guy that mattered. The one who didn't seem to own any clothes that weren't track suits. Vukasin's trigger man. Clearly, he was somebody else's trigger man now.

Even though he'd been there for a lot of the bad business that went down between me and Vukasin, he didn't seem to recognize me now. Or if he did, he didn't care. He looked bored, like he was just passing time while waiting for a bus.

He fired again, but this time he missed, because Vukasin had launched himself at the shooter like a rabid monkey. Grappling and hissing, the two of them crashed into a large glass-front cabinet. The glass shattered and the cabinet tipped, seeming to teeter with indecision before deciding to topple. The room was small and narrow and there was nowhere to get away, so I flattened myself desperately against the back wall. The top corner of the falling cabinet slammed into the left side of my body, causing a bright burst of pain that took my breath away and left me pinned against the wall.

My hearing was still a little iffy from the gunfire, but I was pretty sure I heard other shots coming from the waiting area, along with screaming and swearing. Fragments of the furious exchange between Vukasin and the assassin slipped between the louder sounds like muffled talk radio from a faraway station.

What the fuck was going on here? Some kind of mutiny or power grab that had divided Vukasin's men into sudden violent factions? Was building security involved yet? Cops?

Was Dr. Balian ok? He was a bad lay, but he definitely didn't deserve this kind of action. He wouldn't have needed to operate on Vukasin's dick if Vukasin had never met me. Yet another person whose life was ruined by proximity to me.

There was a confusing, awkward scramble going on, and then another three shots in quick succession. I felt one of them hit the cabinet, the shock reverberating through the metal and my battered body. At least one of the other two hit Vukasin in the face, ending the conversation for good.

There was a weird quiet moment then, a calm bubble in the chaos. Niko got his feet under him and stood in the doorway, gun in hand and evaluating me with those cold eyes. And as I looked at him, he was looking back at me, clearly sizing me up and deciding whether or not to shoot me. I still couldn't tell if he recognized me or not.

He raised the gun, and I felt a sound well up from somewhere inside my aching chest. It wasn't a cry of fear, or desperate pleading or anything like that. It was a strangled, wordless growl of unbearable frustration, like the sound of a trapped animal about to chew its own leg off. I should have been thinking about my own imminent death, but all I could see was Vukasin lying at his feet, dead by someone else's hand. *Not mine*.

I don't know how to make you understand the way that made me feel. Like coitus interruptus. Like I'd spent months building something from scratch with my bare hands and someone just waltzed in and stole it the second before it was finished. Like somebody ate my birthday cake. I'd worked too fucking hard to have it all end like this.

I heard another shot. My whole body clenched in anticipation of a fatal bullet, but I felt nothing. What happened instead was that Niko whipped around, turning his gun to face an unseen assailant in the hallway. More shots, shouting that might have been Croatian, and then he was gone.

I was just frozen there for what felt like ages, trying desperately to hear anything through the ringing in my ears. Nothing.

I steeled myself, bracing for pain, and then shoved the heavy cabinet away with all my strength. It took several tries, the last of which nearly caused me to pass out, but I was finally able to get myself out from under the weight of the cabinet. The pain in my ribs was so intense that I almost didn't notice the jagged dagger of glass sticking out of my forearm. But when that piece of glass banged against the frame of the door, you better fucking believe I noticed. I yanked it out, grunting between clenched teeth, and instantly regretted that decision. The bleeding went from a sluggish trickle to a steady, alarming gush. I tore a piece from Vukasin's hospital gown to wrap around the wound, but the flimsy material was soaked through and useless within seconds. There was no time to search around in the wreckage for gauze or other kinds of bandages. I needed to get the fuck out of there before whatever was happening out in the hallway started happening to me.

5.

Of course, it couldn't be that simple. I probably don't have to tell you what happened next, because if you've spent more than ten seconds on the internet, you already know. But just so the handful of Luddites and hermits and proud dumb-phone users don't feel left out, I'll give you the short version.

I killed a cop. A woman with a new baby, on her first day back on the job after maternity leave. The cold-hearted execution of the saintly victim was captured on surveillance video and quickly went viral, along with calls for swift retribution against the perpetrator. At first, I was just "Unknown Female" but once I had been definitively ID'd by DNA from the generous amount of blood I'd left at the scene, the media circus really kicked into high gear.

But you have to understand, that grainy video fragment is deceptive and doesn't show any of the subtle details of how it really went down.

In the video you see the hero cop lady standing in the center of a long hallway, gun drawn. Low-res, black-and-white, and there's no sound, but you can see a muzzle flash when she fires at a frenetic, blurry whirl of action happening just below the bottom center of the screen.

The next bit has been slowed down and enhanced and played and replayed about a million times. The whirl coalesces into a figure with a gun. A lot of people got distracted by the weird pale blob that flies off to the left side of the screen but that's just the wig.

There's another muzzle flash and the hero cop lady drops.

The gun-wielding figure takes a tentative step towards the fallen cop and then does the thing you're never supposed to do. It looks up at the camera.

I look up at the camera.

That was the moment where so many news broadcasters and internet sleuths froze the video. Me looking right at the fucking camera like I want to make sure everyone gets a real good look at my stupid face. My holy-shit-I-just-shot-a-fucking-cop face.

If you keep watching after that, you'll see me run away down the hallway and disappear into the stairway but there's really no point bothering. Most people who made it that far have already made up their mind about me anyway.

Thing is, they aren't wrong. Not really. But of course, there's more to it than that.

Here's how it actually went down.

When I stumbled out into the hallway, clutching my side with the arm that wasn't bleeding, I nearly tripped over the body of the cute Armenian nurse who had given me the dirty look. The older man I'd accidentally walked in on earlier was running down the hall swearing vociferously, gown flapping wide open in the back to expose his bony ass and low slung nutsack. No sign of Balian. I was feeling panicky and disoriented, and it took me a second to remember the location of the impossibly distant exit.

That's when I found myself suddenly and intimately acquainted with one of Vukasin's other thugs.

This guy was one of the interchangeable meatheads who composed his rotating entourage of low-rent knee-breakers. There were five total, usually only two or three on shift at any given time. They were steroid-swollen Ken dolls, tough to tell apart. Especially when I only had eyes for Vukasin. Of the five, there was only one blond. This guy was not the blond.

He was leaning against the wall, face gone pasty gray under his dark stubble and looking like he was maybe about to puke. His white shirt was tie-dyed with gore, but it was hard to tell how much of it was his. At least some of it clearly was, as evidenced by the steady trickle of fresh red blood leaking from his left pant leg and ruining his pricy kicks.

He said something to me in slushy Croatian and then lunged at me way faster than I would have expected from someone in his condition, dragging me into a weird half-hug half-chokehold, like a drowning man. I silently struggled and kicked against him, desperate to get away from him and his personal olfactory weather system of fear-sweat and blood and Drakkar Noir. It felt kinda like dealing with your friend who's drunk and really, *really* loves you but also has a gun and wants to kill you.

The gun went off right by my head. I wrenched my head and upper body backward and away, crooked wig flying off in the process. I was already half deaf from the previous gunfire, but all I could hear after that was the muffled thump of my terrified heart beating like a techno baseline under the harsh tinny ringing. I thought maybe people were shouting, but it just sounded like distant rumbling. I could feel the guy's whole body weakening against me and I was concentrating on trying to peel his thick hairy fingers off the gun.

Then someone shot at me.

I will never claim to be any kind of quick-draw marksman or anything like that. I've used guns for their intended purpose a lot more often than I've liked and occasionally succeeded in shooting one of my fellow humans, but they still feel a little weird in my hand. Like a highly specialized piece of sports equipment for a game I don't really like or understand. But somehow, the one time in my life when I really should have missed, when I needed to miss, I didn't.

I felt an electric jolt of terrified adrenaline as I spun towards the new and unknown threat with the thug's gun in my hand, squeezing the trigger before my eyes could even register who it was that shot at me.

By all laws of physics, that wild, hail-Mary bullet should have plowed into the acoustic tile ceiling, or the colorful poster reminding men to have regular screenings for prostate cancer, or the cart full of catheters and syringes. But it didn't. It hit the hero cop lady in her muscular inner thigh, severing her femoral artery and releasing all the blood in her body in a sudden, high-velocity geyser not unlike a shaken bottle of champagne.

I locked eyes with her as she realized what had happened. She looked scared, and that was so much worse than if she was glaring at me or hating me in that moment. I was overwhelmed with this desire to mouth the word *sorry,* but I was just frozen there, staring at her. Then her face went gray and slack, eyes rolling back as she ragdolled into a bloody heap.

I took a tentative step towards the dying cop and then remembered the security camera.

I had noted it when I first started visiting the doc at his office. It wasn't the only one in the practice. There were none in the exam rooms, obviously, just the one over the reception desk and this one in the hall, facing the back door. It was small and subtle and might not even be noticed by anyone less paranoid than me. Which was intentional, since most guys wouldn't like the idea of being caught on camera visiting a urologist who also specializes in surgical solutions for erectile dysfunction and reconstructive and cosmetic procedures for male genitalia.

Of course, I'd factored in the existence of that camera when I was gaming out my plan to kill Vukasin. I knew there was no way to avoid being seen going in and out even without the camera there. But with my big blond wig and heavy makeup, I felt safe in the knowledge that I'd be remembered the wrong way. That

I could shed my trashy blonde stranger's skin in a nearby parking lot and walk away as a completely different person.

In the thick of the messy, terrifying and unexpected chaos that had erupted in the wake of my failed assassination attempt, I hadn't been thinking about anything but getting out alive. Then, when I saw the cop go down, I suddenly remembered the camera. I should have just hunched down and covered my face as I hustled out but for some reason the act of remembering the camera pulled my face up towards it like a magnet. Like I had to check to make sure it was still there or something. Anyway, I have no excuse. I did a stupid thing. And I'm currently fucked because of it.

6.

I pulled into a corner mini-mall parking lot and eased the stolen car into a slot in front of a liquor store. There was a sign that warned me not to park there for more than five minutes. Wise advice.

The adrenaline was wearing off and pain was kicking in. The worst of it was on the left side of my body, a hot pulse that reached a shrill, stabbing crescendo at the top of each breath. I had planned to strip out of the scrubs in the car, but I quickly realized that I was unable to raise my arms to pull off the top without excruciating pain. I wound up zipping a black hoodie over the bloody top and swapping the scrub pants for the forgettable gray jersey maxiskirt I had packed and ready. I did my best to stick with the steps of my plan, scrubbing away the heavy makeup with a handful of moist wipes and removing the disposable blue contacts, but inside I was panicking and sure that everyone around was watching me.

I went to get out of the car and throw the bag of incriminating items into the liquor store trash, but the massive wave of agony and dizziness that hit when I tried to stand wrenched an embarrassingly loud shriek out from between my clenched teeth. If people weren't really watching me before, they were now.

The sleeve of my hoodie was already soaked through from the unchecked flow of blood, and I was pretty sure it wasn't gonna stop without some stitches. Never mind the probably broken rib that felt like it was stabbing me in the lung with every breath. It was the last thing I wanted to do, but it was looking like I had no choice but to get myself to some kind of doctor before I bled out like that dead cop I didn't want to think about.

L.A. traffic is never fun, but it's even less fun when you're beaten, bruised and bleeding to death, trying to drive yourself to the hospital before you black out behind the wheel.

Of course, I drove right past Cedar Sinai. I didn't want expensive, quality care. I needed stressed-out, sleepless interns desperately treading water in a sea of gang violence, drug casualties and mental health crises.

East Central Care Clinic was exactly what I needed.

It was a lot like getting stitches at the DMV. Endless lines, fraying nerves, exasperated and underpaid employees. There were feverish kids crying in the waiting room and some adults too. An elderly woman was laid out on the grimy green linoleum floor with her face pressed against the far wall underneath a wilted cardboard sombrero and a crooked sign wishing everyone a happy Cinco de Mayo. When I asked the triage nurse if the woman was ok, he said she did that every single day. The whole place smelled of ammonia and despair. It took me over an hour to get the stitches, by which time I'd lost so much blood that I could no longer stand without assistance. I had to be put in a wheelchair to go get my chest x-ray.

I had completely forgotten about the whole pregnancy thing until I saw that familiar sign on the wall, the one we've all seen a million times and yet never paid any attention. At least I never did until that day.

Please inform technician if you are or think you might be pregnant.

Shit.

The technician was a no-nonsense Latina with a build like an Olympic swimmer and shrewd dark eyes.

"Ok, listen I…um," I said, trying not to stammer like a lying child and failing miserably. "Well, I think…I might be pregnant. I mean, probably not but…is there…like a test you can give me, or…"

She gave me a silently annoyed now-you-tell-me expression then turned and left the x-ray room without a single word, leaving me alone and feeling stupid.

Being left alone with my thoughts was the last thing I needed.

I probably should have been thinking about this whole potential pregnancy situation, but my mind kept replaying Vukasin's death over and over. How my victory, my closure, the whole purpose of what I had left of a life had been snatched from me by someone who could not have cared less. Who was just doing his job. I should have been happy the fucker was dead, but it felt so unfair. Killing him was the only thing left to get me out of bed in the mornings. Now what?

After what felt like hours of that private hell, a new nurse appeared, an older black woman with salt-and-pepper natural hair, cheerful pink leopard glasses and a gentle demeanor. She wheeled me down the hall to a claustrophobic room full of creepy posters showing cutaway pregnant bellies and fetuses in various stages of development.

"Listen," I said as she helped me from the chair onto a gyno-style exam table. "I just had a period like two weeks ago, but I've got this…fluid coming out of my nipples."

"Ok, let's have a look," she replied, peeling down my paper gown.

When she gently squeezed one of my nipples, it oozed more of that pearly yellow stuff. She smiled. I felt sick to my stomach.

"Well, you're definitely producing colostrum," she said. "Can you lay back for me?"

She helped me lean back, gritting my teeth against the grinding pain in my ribs until I was flat on my back. My whole body felt iced with dread.

She pushed the gown up over my belly and laid a folded blue paper covering over my crotch.

"How long have you had this dark line under your navel?"

I figured it was a bad idea to tell her that I'd been too busy plotting a murder to waste time navel-gazing, so I just shrugged.

"When did you say you had your last period?"

"A few weeks ago," I said.

"Are you sure?"

"Yes," I replied. The ocean of dread was threatening to drown me. Was I? Was I really sure of anything anymore?

Her warm, gentle hands moved over the shape of my belly.

"I'd like to do a quick ultrasound, ok?"

I felt like a corpse on an autopsy table as she squirted cold gel onto my clammy skin. I couldn't move, couldn't speak. I just stared at the dusty, crooked acoustic tile ceiling above me, dis-associating as she started rolling that hard wand around on my belly.

"Well, Lucy," she said. "You were right. You are definitely pregnant. Everything looks normal and it doesn't seem like your baby has suffered any obvious trauma from your accident. Would you like to see?"

I'd forgotten the fake name I gave the front desk and so for a second, I was sure she was talking to someone else. When she just stood there, waiting for my response, I blurted out:

"Fuck, I can't…I mean…I have to get rid of it."

She paused like she was carefully planning what to say next and I thought for a moment she was about to give me some religious argument about how abortion is murder. What she actually said turned out to be so much worse.

"Lucy, listen to me," she said. "According to my measurements, you are approximately twenty-eight weeks in. That's the end of the second trimester. Abortion is not impossible at this point, but it's a lot more complicated this late into a pregnancy. Of course there are other options if you are not able to..."

"Wait, wait, twenty-eight weeks?" I cut her off, overloaded brain still struggling with the math. "What is that six...no, seven months?"

"Approximately."

"No, that's not possible," I said. "I've had my period. More than once. It's always been kinda light and never exactly regular but..."

"Breakthrough bleeding that occurs during pregnancy can mimic normal menstruation and, in many cases..."

She was going on and on, but I could no longer hear her words, because I'd done some other math inside my head, counting back twenty-nine weeks and change. Remembering reckless, unprotected sex in the back of a stolen car in the Mexican desert.

Cody. Jesus.

I had been certain I was going to die that night, and I ended up making a new person instead. Too bad for it, considering every other person who had the rotten luck of getting mixed up with me was now dead. Including its father.

She wiped the goo off my abdomen and helped me to sit up. I was unable to suppress a breathless yelp, clutching at the blooming bruises under my left armpit.

"Don't take this the wrong way," she said. "But I'm legally required to ask." She took both my hands in hers, trying to look into my skittish eyes. "Do you feel unsafe in your current home environment, Lucy?"

I didn't mean to laugh and tried too late to swallow the bitter chuckle that burbled up like acid in my throat. I didn't know what was funnier, the idea that I had a home environment or the idea that I would ever be safe again.

"I honestly have no idea what that even means," I told her.

Her expression was sad and knowing and she nodded silently, squeezing my hands.

"Ok," she said. "Let's get you taken care of first, and then we can go over your options."

She gave me a handful of pamphlets with information I didn't want to know and moved me into a different room where I was supposed to wait for more tests and referrals. I didn't. I couldn't.

What if she felt a moral duty to help the poor beat-up pregnant lady and got the police involved?

I left.

7.

You know when you find out someone you love has been lying to you, and all of a sudden, a bunch of things that seemed a little off actually make perfect sense? That's what it felt like, lying sleepless and unable to get comfortable in my latest hotel bed, going over all the hints that added up to the horrifying and inescapable truth of my current situation.

The lumpy and unlovely weight gain around my middle.

The perpetual, anxious queasiness I wrote off as nerves.

The fact that I couldn't stomach any food other than French fries, which didn't seem that important because it was easier to go through the drive-through and eat in my car while I was tailing Vukasin across Los Angeles.

That bloated uncomfortable brick in my belly that I figured was just constipation from all those late-night French fries.

The disconcerting sensation of movement deep in my guts that wasn't cramps or gas pains after all.

I felt that strange, alien movement again, like somehow the little living thing inside me knew that I was thinking about it. About how it was now too big to be aborted with suction alone and would have to be chopped into pieces. About how I felt when I watched its father die. I'd seen so much death, caused so much death. Did one more death really matter?

I couldn't answer that question, but I couldn't make myself get an abortion either.

I told myself I'd deal with that situation later, once I had some kind of plan for coping with the more pressing issue of being a high-profile cop killer on the lam with a bunch of pissed-off Croatians who probably wanted me dead.

That's how I thought of the pregnancy. Not as a baby, or my baby or anything like that. Just *The Situation*.

I wish I could tell you that I put a clever plan together and took action right away. That's what the old Angel would have done, but I didn't and I'm still not sure why not. What I did instead was post an ad offering preggo fetish sessions. Just to help me save up a little extra cash while I figured out what to do next.

8.

My Husband Doesn't Know! That was the title of my ad. Also my excuse for why I had to hide my identity with different wigs and sunglasses. Guys didn't give a shit. They weren't paying to look at my face anyway.

I was deliberately avoiding reading any detailed information about pregnancy or childbirth, because that would somehow validate the Situation as something more than just a fetish. But there were some things I couldn't avoid learning from clients.

The first thing I learned was to lie about how pregnant I was. The farther along you are, the more you can charge, but I'd had more than one client walk out on me because my belly didn't look big enough so I just stuck with saying six months. At least it was easy to remember. The second thing I learned was that I was expected to pack a powerful olfactory wallop, so washing up before a client was a no-no. But in the end, my breasts were my biggest moneymakers. My uneven and undersized belly might have been inadequate for some guys, but my swollen, leaky tits more than made up for it.

I was getting by, getting through each day without killing anybody or being arrested, but I was not ok. I was broken.

Loneliness does weird things to your brain. Back when I still had my hatred of Vukasin driving me like a jet engine, I felt like he was always with me. There was a strange comfort in knowing that he was out there hating me as much as I hated him.

I missed him.

I know that sounds utterly fucked up, but it's true. It felt like he was the last person on earth who knew the real me and now that he was dead, there was nothing left between me and that vast sea of loneliness. Even though I had a brand-new human developing inside me, one who really was always with me, I somehow felt more isolated than ever.

I felt alone in the supermarket as I tried to convince myself to buy vegetables this time and not the starchy junk food I knew I'd get instead. I felt alone sitting in a grungy internet café compulsively reading through the thousands of posts calling for my rape, torture and death. I felt alone with a stranger's dick in my mouth or between my oozing breasts. The only time I didn't feel alone was when I felt paranoid, convinced that someone had recognized me. The surly cops at the hamburger stand, maybe, or that girl who looked like she might be in the business, or the guy staring right at me while talking softly into his cell phone.

Week after week disappeared into that vortex of loneliness, punctuated by occasional spikes of existential terror. I felt messy, hideous, perpetually on the brink of some kind of humiliating meltdown. I cried and punched walls and stared into space. I used my vibrator so often that my occupied uterus must have felt like a cheap apartment near LAX.

I kept thinking about the husband of my victim, also a cop and holding his baby in a press conference video I must have watched a hundred times. His name was Bill Corbin, a skinny guy with thick brown wolfman hair and sleepless, anguished eyes. His uniform shirt was incorrectly buttoned. A single father now, telling the cameras that the monster who ruined their lives and took away his son's mother didn't deserve to live.

He wasn't wrong, but honestly, he could get in line behind all the other people whose lives I ruined. Including my own.

I didn't have anywhere to go, so I drifted in aimless circles. I used stolen cars to travel between forgettable suburban locations.

Between the pain of my healing ribs and the discomfort of my growing belly, I barely slept. When I did, my dreams were filled with dead men's faces and the smell of burning duct tape. I spent long restless nights in bland, mid-range hotel rooms paid for by johns, eating too many minibar snacks and binge-watching home improvement shows.

I couldn't stand to watch anything where people were angry or yelling, not even a comedy. I found myself craving the predictability and soothing blandness of a world where the only conflict that existed was over which tile to choose for the backsplash or whether to go with move-in-ready or a fixer-upper. But then some small throwaway moment in one of those shows would leave me sobbing inconsolably, missing my little house so badly it felt like mourning yet another murdered lover.

Really, I missed the old me. The me that I would never be again.

I got up every morning with a panicky determination to act, to move, to find a way to escape from the brain-numbing inertia and be the strong, decisive person I always believed I was. But then somehow each day would slip through my fingers with nothing done and nothing changed. I knew there was an unavoidable and rapidly approaching deadline on the Situation, but I kept telling myself I just needed to save up a few more bucks. I just needed to give the Twitter mob thing a little more time to die down and move on to its next target. I just needed to see if this nice gay couple decided on the mid-century with the pool or the historic Victorian.

In the end, the decision to hit the road was made for me.

9.

The guy said his name was Jim, but he was Italian so that seemed like an odd choice. From Italy Italian, not Italian American, like me. His English was fluent but strongly accented and he was decent looking in a slouchy, bearded, pretentious artist kind of way. Light brown hair expensively styled to look like he woke up like that. Stiff Japanese selvedge jeans. Mean blue eyes that I ignored because I was too busy looking at the fan of hundreds in his hand.

He didn't want any of the more esoteric fetish stuff, he just wanted to fuck. Worse, he wanted missionary. Normally if johns wanted to fuck, I made them do it doggy style because it was easier to zone out and ignore them and because I got a tiny sliver of passive-aggressive satisfaction out of knowing they had to stare at my pregnancy-induced hemorrhoids while they did it.

This guy had a big dick too, and I was concentrating so hard on not screaming out loud as it slammed over and over into my hyper-sensitive cervix that I didn't notice his raised hand until it cracked against my sweaty cheek.

"Fuck you," I said, shoving him away from me and struggling to close my knees. "We're done, asshole."

He smiled at me, the way someone might smile at a puppy that is being a little bit naughty, but in a cute way.

Then his hand clamped down on my neck, squeezing my breath down to nothing while he playfully slapped at both sides of my face with the other hand. He was saying something in Italian, but much to my Nonna Vincenza's dismay, I don't know any words for things that aren't food. It was obvious that he wasn't talking about food.

I'd like to say that I snapped or lost control or something, but that's not how it was at all. It was more like I became the truest, most distilled version of myself in that moment. As if I breathed myself in like the last gasp of oxygen before a deep dive and let that truest version of me fill up all the hollow spaces in my body. Then I killed him.

I'm not proud of what I did. It was messy and stupid and ultimately unnecessary, but I couldn't stop myself.

I grabbed the pinkie of the hand on my neck and cranked it up and backward until he lost his grip while I got my legs between us and dug my bare feet into his soft belly. Then I shoved him away with all my strength, which somehow seemed to be way more than I had expected. He obviously wasn't expecting it either, judging by the expression on his face as he staggered backwards and plopped awkwardly down on his butt, dick bouncing comically against the shitty hotel carpet.

I suppose I could have done a lot of different things at that point. I could have run away. I could have locked myself in the bathroom and hoped that he'd cut his losses and fuck off. I could have called the hotel security guy that I blew in exchange for bouncing problem clients without asking any questions or getting the cops involved.

What I did was kill the guy with an ugly lamp. It was modern and heavy, with a rectangular base that looked kind of like a fancy concrete block. The nubbly oatmeal linen shade fell off pretty much right away, but the cord stayed attached, whipping around me when it popped out of the wall socket. The shape of the base was unwieldy and nothing like a weapon, but I didn't give a shit. I just dug my fingers into the geometric holes and hung on to it as best I could while I smashed him in the face with it. A lot.

That was the first time that I really felt pregnant.

When the rage wore off and I started to notice the torn skin on my fingers and the deep ache in my arms, shoulders and ribs, I let the lamp base fall to the bloody carpet and turned away from the mess I had made. I rushed to the john, thinking I might puke, but somehow managed not to. It seemed like a small victory.

I didn't look at myself in the mirror while I rinsed the worst of the blood from my face and hair. Another victory, given how bad I probably looked. The water was cold and bracing and my breathing started to slow down to something near normal. Of course, that didn't last.

There was somebody at the door. The wrong somebody.

A series of knocks, normal first, then louder, more fist than knuckles. Then, a woman's calm, steady voice.

"Security," said the woman who wasn't the security guy I blew. Just my fucking luck. "Everything ok in there?"

Everything was not ok. My heart felt like it was gonna take off without me already and when I heard the beep of the electronic lock trying to disengage, I figured I'd better catch up.

10.

I grabbed the complimentary hotel robe, tied it around my belly as best I could and took rapid-fire stock of my options, ranging from terrible to impossible. I could hear an unfamiliar male voice outside the door saying *Try it again* and I knew I was out of time five minutes ago, so I picked the stubby little balcony. The lesser evil, or at least that's what I told myself as I slid the glass door closed behind me as quietly as possible and hoped that the weighty blackout curtains had time to settle before the people on the other side of the door came in and saw the mess I'd left for them.

I pressed myself against the grungy stucco, trying to catch my breath. The balcony had a single metal chair and a rickety little table, neither one of which was anywhere near large enough to hide a homicidal pregnant lady. I knew it wouldn't be long before the people in the room shoved back the curtains and saw me, so I had no choice but to clamber over to the neighboring balcony, silently thanking the dead guy for being too cheap to pay the fifty bucks extra for a "view suite" on a higher floor.

Easier said than done.

I was on the third floor. Way too high to jump down onto the concrete without severely fucking myself up, but not so high that I would definitely die if I fell. At least, that's what I told myself.

The balcony looked out over the busy street in front rather than the parking lot in back. In typical Southern California fashion, there was the perpetual claim that you could maybe see the ocean if you climbed high enough or paid enough, but definitely not from down here. Back when this hotel had been built, sometime around when I was shooting my first boy/girl scene from the look of it, there must have been a view of the narrow, anemic park that continued down the other side of the street to the right. Now there was just a big, dusty construction project and the only view was of palm tree stumps, chain-link and the backed-up freeway beyond. I had no choice but to add my ass to that list and hope everyone was too busy being annoyed about the traffic to bother looking up my flapping bathrobe as I threw one puffy, swollen foot over the rail.

I hoisted my bulk up so that I was kind of half straddling the rail and took stock of the situation. There was a thick wall between the balconies that gave each one an illusion of privacy, so it would be a bit of a stretch to get from the railing on my side to the railing on the other. Balancing like this was excruciatingly uncomfortable and I could hear shouting now from inside in the room, so I let myself down as quickly as I could manage on the outside of the railing and started inching over to the wall between the balconies.

I joke that my life had become a bad action movie, but if that were actually true, I would have been doing cool, acrobatic moves and flying gracefully on a wire at this point, preferably in a sexy leather catsuit and heels. Also not pregnant, probably.

In my actual life, I reached over to the other railing with an unlovely grunt, smooshed my belly and tits against the rough edge of the stucco wall, then closed my eyes and took that wide, wobbly step onto the lip of the neighboring balcony.

I hauled myself up and over the railing and flattened my extremely-not-flat body as much as possible against the wall, desperately trying to silence my embarrassing panting and gasping.

The glass door to this room was slightly open.

The curtains were closed but drifting hypnotically in and out on the tide of air-conditioning from the cold, dark interior. There was clearly someone in there. Why else would the door be open?

I thought for a second that I should keep moving, keep climbing along the front-facing balconies until I found an unoccupied room. But a room with nobody inside would probably be locked and anyway, I could hear the glass door to my room sliding open and then that female voice asking her companion if he saw anyone. He certainly would if I tried to keep on climbing around like the world's most ungainly ninja. I had no choice but to take my chances with whoever was inside that room.

The door was only partway open and there was something blocking it from opening any wider, so I had to squeeze and wriggle in through the narrow gap.

Let's not dwell on the part where I got kinda stuck. Just for a second. A panicky, end of the fucking world second where I was sure I would be caught because of my big stupid belly. The Situation didn't appreciate being squashed like that, but it probably wouldn't have appreciated being born in prison either, so we both just had to suck it up and get the hell out of sight.

Inside the room it was dark and smelled like a bar. It took a second for my eyes to adjust to the gloom but when I did, I saw a naked blonde sacked out horizontally across the bed. She still had on a full face of hi-def TV makeup and was deeply tanned and ferociously skinny. One of her navy pumps was still on and the other had been kicked off with such velocity that it had left a scuff on the wall before landing in the plastic ice bucket. Her overflowing suitcase was what had been blocking the sliding door from opening any wider.

I slid the door closed as quietly as I could and then pressed my ear to the wall, trying to hear what was happening next door over the blonde's soft, fluttering snores. All I could hear was muffled voices, but I couldn't make out what they were saying.

I rifled through her spilled clothing for something less conspicuous than the bathrobe, but none of those tiny, jewel-toned sheath dresses and narrow stiletto heels were going to work. I was looking around for a handbag or wallet when there was a knock on her door. I ducked into the dark bathroom while the blonde rolled onto her stomach and pulled a pillow over her head.

"NO MAID POR FAVOR!" she yelled, her husky voice muffled and slurry.

The knocking continued as I stepped cautiously into the bathtub and pulled the shower curtain closed.

"Hotel security!" The same voice that had been at my door minutes before. "Can you come to the door, ma'am?"

I knew that kind of ma'am. That cop ma'am that had nothing to do with conferring respect. That kind of ma'am meant you better fucking do what they say or they'll shoot you and call it self-defense.

The blonde clearly did not know what that kind of ma'am meant.

"Are you fucking kidding me right now?" she was asking as she stumbled and fumbled around noisily, presumably putting on one of those tube-sock-sized dresses. "Do you have any idea who I am?"

I heard the door to the room open.

"Is there anyone else in there with you?"

"What are you implying? Do you not see this ring?"

I wished that I could use this distraction to sneak away, but there was no other way out of the room. I was trapped until the security people decided to move on.

The blonde continued berating them and scoffing at their questions while I tried to come up with any kind of fucking scenario in which I could get out of this bathroom unnoticed. My only hope would be for her to pass back out, which was seeming less and less likely the more agitated she became. I eyed the toilet through the gap at one end of the shower curtain, desperately wondering if anybody would notice if I took a really quick piss. My bladder felt like the floor of a bouncy castle, but hey, if I couldn't hold it, at least I was inside the bathtub.

I guess I wasn't the only one thinking about pissing because the blonde abruptly slammed the door in the faces of the inquisitive security people and came barging into the bathroom, swearing under her breath.

I pressed myself into the cold tile and held my breath as I listened to her unleash an aggressively powerful stream of urine that went on and on for what felt like hours. Cruel and unusual punishment in my current condition.

Then she flushed, but I didn't hear the water running in the sink. Either she was just sitting there, or else she was doing something that didn't make any sound. When a bright flash went off, I flinched.

She was taking selfies. Hopefully not on the toilet.

That seemed funny in an awful sort of way, and I almost laughed out loud before I could stop myself, but then my body was suddenly iced with cold, clammy sweat and my heart was beating so hard it hurt. The camera on the woman's phone flashed and flashed again and I had to get the fuck out of there, but I couldn't. I couldn't.

I think I can make video on my phone, Vukasin said.

I couldn't possibly be smelling burning duct tape, except somehow, I was, along with that fucking peppermint gum and I was gonna puke or scream or kill that woman with my bare hands and damn the consequences.

I didn't do any of those things. I waited.

Eventually, she got the shot she wanted and left the bathroom.

I stayed in the bathtub for way too long, listening with my whole body, but everything was quiet. Did she leave the hotel room? Was she asleep again? Was she sitting there silently waiting for me to come out so she could tackle me and call the cops?

When I finally got up the courage to creep over to the partially closed bathroom door, I saw her curled up under the covers, facing away so just the tangled crown of her blonde head was visible.

I moved as silently as I could, holding both my breath and my aching bladder, and made my way around her scattered belongings, over towards that ice bucket. I removed her wet shoe from the bucket and emptied the meltwater out onto the carpet without ever taking my eyes off her. She shifted her legs once and just about gave me a heart attack, but she never woke up.

I eased the door open, peering out through my sweaty hair to scope the hallway. The security people were at the opposite end, revealed now as an unlikely pair in cheap gray uniforms. The woman was tall and thin with a tight bun and a razor-sharp profile, and the man was short and stocky with a shaved head and a reddish beard. They were talking to somebody I couldn't see, somebody who sounded only slightly less annoyed than the blonde had been, and I didn't have much time to make my move. I tucked the empty ice bucket under my arm and strolled casually down the hall towards the ice machine. I remembered my own mother telling me that she had chewed ice cubes during her pregnancies and had that excuse in the chamber ready to use on anyone who tried to talk to me. Luckily, I didn't end up needing it and was able to duck unnoticed into the stairway.

I may or may not have left that ice bucket full of piss on the second-floor landing before beating it out the back door to the parking lot.

As I cautiously pushed the heavy door open, I saw two crooked, hastily parked prowl cars with their bar lights on. There were four cops shoving their way into the main back entrance. Real police, not dollar store rent-a-cops like the security guards I'd seen up on the third floor. Three men and a woman and they all had deadly serious expressions and black ribbons across the faces of their badges.

Those ribbons could have been for any reason at all. L.A. was huge, and lots of cops got killed. There was no way to know if they were for the particular cop I killed.

Except I knew.

I didn't turn myself in, though. I waited until they were inside and then I ran.

Running through the city with bare feet sucks, by the way.

11.

There was a 24-hour gym a couple of doors down from the hotel. A popular chain with an angry red logo and a big parking structure in back. I ducked into the parking structure and positioned my sweaty, panting, bathrobe-clad bulk behind a forgettable little gray Toyota to watch the exit.

Upside to a gym, most people going in or out will have a change of clothes. Downside, most of them can kick your ass if you try to take their gym bag. This wasn't a very well thought out plan, but it was all I had so I watched and waited.

A handful of fit, healthy people passed by me, oblivious, bopping to whatever was playing through their sporty, sweat-proof earbuds. A black guy with designer glasses and a Batman shirt. A Middle Eastern girl, young and pretty with a long, thick ponytail that brushed the top of her squat-sculpted ass as she walked. An older bodybuilder type, blonde with big, shrink-wrapped breast implants and a leathery tan. Even her hair looked thirsty.

I was starting to doubt my plan, such as it was. I felt scattered, nauseous, still shaking from adrenaline and suddenly the choice of which person's gym bag I should snatch seemed overwhelming, an impossible calculation that would inevitably be wrong. Wrong, with dire fucking consequences.

Suddenly, it seemed like the best plan in the world was to find an unlocked car and curl up in the back seat. A nap, that was the answer. Just a short one.

Really, would jail be that bad?

The next guy was the right guy.

He was clearly new to this whole going-to-the-gym thing. I could tell by his pristine leather duffel bag with the lurid logo of a fight promotion combined with his soft, fast-food physique. He had pale hair with a wiry, rebellious curl and skim-milk-colored skin that looked grown in a lab under 24-hour fluorescent lighting. You don't see a lot of that kind of sunless pallor in Southern California.

Best of all, we were about the same size and shape. Belly included.

I opened up the top of the robe until my tits were almost falling out, hoping they would short circuit any questions or common-sense reasons to get the hell away from this crazy woman.

I tried to put a little sexy in my walk as I strolled over to him, but my bare swollen feet hurt so bad I probably looked more like a chubby dog wearing snow boots for the first time. But thankfully, my tits did their job. His gaze went right to them.

"Hi," I said, like it was totally normal for me to be barefoot in a bathrobe in the gym parking lot. "Your bag is so cool. Where did you get it?"

"Um," he said to my tits. "Online."

"Can I see it?"

"Okay." He held the bag out to me, eyes locked on target.

I grabbed the bag and took off.

"Sorry!" I yelled back over my shoulder.

He didn't chase after me. He just stood there with his cheeks all pinked up and staring at his feet with a slump-shouldered and defeated posture. Like this kind of thing happened to him all the time.

"Damn," he said, almost too soft to hear.

I felt terrible, but I didn't give him his bag back.

*

After half-running, then fast walking, then sort of waddling in a zigzag pattern through side streets and alleys with my hip joints on fire, I finally found a relatively sheltered corner behind a 7-Eleven dumpster. It was already occupied by a snoring, vaguely human shape in a sleeping bag, but that person didn't seem to mind sharing, or even be aware of my momentary intrusion.

I swiftly inventoried the contents of the bag. No money, credit cards, keys or phone. Just some brand-new sweatpants, a brand-new t-shirt with the same logo as the bag, a brand-new pair of gratuitously expensive running shoes and a brand-new stainless-steel water bottle, currently empty, except for a small piece of paper advising me not to put it in the dishwasher. There was a rattling noise coming from somewhere in the bag, but it took me a second to find the inner pocket containing several bottles of dubious-looking supplements. Still no money.

The clothes fit, as long as I let my belly hang over the drawstring waistband. The sneakers did not, not even close. They were both too big and too narrow, but they were better than barefoot, so they would have to do for now. I left the bag and the supplements with the sleeping person, figuring whoever they were, they could probably use the Super XXX TestoBoost pills more than I could.

It wasn't until after I had given the gym bag away, that it hit me that my own bag was back at the hotel, its contents waiting to be analyzed and processed into some police evidence locker downtown. I didn't give a shit about my spare cotton panties and cheap maternity leggings. It would have been nice to have the cash and the prepaid Visa cards and the burner phone, but there was really only one thing it hurt to lose.

The drawing. The drawing of a dead man.

I suppose I owe you a little backstory at this point.

12.

Don't you hate when somebody goes off on a whole long, complicated tangent about an obscure TV show from their childhood that they can't quite remember?

You know, the one where…

I hate it too, but indulge me in a quick lightning round of exactly that.

Let's start with the one where the semi-retired porn star has this amazing life and owns her own house and her own business but then she gets left for dead in the trunk of an abandoned car.

The one where she gets mixed up in a human trafficking ring and gets her best friend Didi killed while trying to figure out how to get revenge against the guys who were responsible for that whole trunk thing.

Or how about the one where she promised to help and protect a dying friend's eighteen-year-old son, Cody, but wound up getting pregnant and getting him killed.

The one where she got help from an old punch-drunk fighter named Hank and definitely didn't have any kind of feelings about him, which is probably for the best because she got him killed too.

No wonder that show got canceled. Too depressing.

In retrospect, it's hard to believe that really there was a time when the most pressing issue on my mind was whether or not to get my middle-aged tits surgically perked up. If only back-then me could see these nutritious and delicious 32Gs currently stretching my stolen t-shirt to its absolute limit.

Lucky for me, men could see them just fine. Specifically, men with cars.

A heavily tattooed guy named Emmanuel gave me a lift to Rancho Mirage in his un-air-conditioned Mazda. There wasn't really enough room in the back seat for him to fuck my tits like he wanted so we had to do it on the side of the road with the door open for cover. He knew a gas station that had really good Punjabi food and gave me a new shirt, an extra-large green t-shirt from his fence-rental company that had never been worn.

A guy who went by Junior but seemed way too old for that name took me to Calexico and didn't want anything in return.

By then it was dark and I didn't want to be hanging around with my thumb out like I was fishing for serial killers, so I stole a Kia that somebody left running in a strip-club parking lot. It smelled like baby oil and cigarettes and had three quarters of a tank of gas. I figured it was a good bet but it broke down on me after less than twenty minutes on the road.

The trucker who stopped for me was named Dave and wasn't a serial killer. He took me the rest of the way to my destination. For a reasonable price, of course.

13.

Dave the trucker dropped me off by the Sierra Sands golf course sign in the suburbs of Yuma, AZ. Some clever young artiste had drawn a dick and balls on the lower left-hand corner of the sign, positioned as if attempting to penetrate the second capital S.

Nothing much had really changed since my last visit to Nine Iron Drive, but yet it felt like everything had changed. Bland, normal houses seemed sinister, filled with unseen watchers. I found myself getting turned around and inexplicably lost. I became increasingly convinced that the little Spanish-style house with the saguaro cactus sign had never really existed. That Hank never really existed. That Angel never existed.

But then suddenly, there it was, all alone on its empty, undeveloped dead-end street. The cute succulent garden. The cactus sign that read WYMAN & CARR. A warm, diffuse glow from the front windows, filtered through sheer curtains. It was probably too late to knock, but I did anyway.

Wyman answered the door in a plaid flannel bathrobe over faded blue pajamas. He had clearly put his toupee on quickly and without a mirror, so it sat at an oddly jaunty angle, like a cocked hat.

"Angel?" he said, blinking incredulously behind his thick glasses.

I had spent a lot of time composing what I would say to him, how I would present my torturous and ever-evolving story in a way that would make him want to help me. That all went out the window and I dissolved into a sobbing puddle of hormones.

"Oh, honey," he said softly, taking both of my shaking hands. "Come inside."

He deposited me onto a soft brown leather sofa and started bustling around in the open kitchen, although really bustling is the wrong word. Now that I was getting a good look at him, he appeared to have aged a decade since the last time I saw him. He seemed so frail and small as he clung to the edges of the marble countertop, working his way around a kettle and cabinets like he was in a ship's galley on choppy seas.

"I hope you'll forgive the state of the place," he said. "I don't seem to be able to keep on top of the chores as well these days and my helper isn't due until tomorrow."

The room was the same as I remembered. Same rugged cowboy paintings. Same fat orange cat. Same fireplace with the same faded photo of two smiling young men on the mantel. But everything did seem a little shabbier. Cat hair and dust bunnies gathered in corners. Loose threads hung from stained throw pillows and a smell of medicine and unwashed clothes mingled with a faint air of cat litter.

After months in the soulless liminal spaces of forgettable hotels, it all seemed wonderful to me, like a real home. Being in a familiar home with somebody who knew who I was made me feel real again. I wanted to stay there with him forever.

"You look like you could use a stiff drink," he said, carefully unwrapping a tea bag with delicate, knobby fingers. "We both could, honestly, but I don't think that would be a good idea for either one of us. Chamomile tea it is!"

He shuffled over to me with a chunky pottery cup in each hand, gave me one and then sat down beside me.

"It doesn't taste like much of anything, honestly, but if you put enough honey in there it's not too bad."

It felt warm and smelled nice and that started the water-works again. Really, I was a total useless wreck.

"You want to tell me about it?" he asked.

I didn't want to, honestly, but I did.

"I see," he said after a long pause and a sip of tea. "Is the baby Hank's?"

I couldn't make myself lie out loud, so I just nodded. I don't have any idea why I didn't want to tell him the truth in that moment. Maybe that's what I wanted to be true.

"What are you going to do?" he asked.

"Good fucking question," I said. "I was thinking of maybe going south and hoping you might still have the template for the ID you made me."

"Sadly, no," he said. "I scrubbed all that stuff from my drives after, well, you know..."

I knew. I sipped my tea.

"I didn't mean to kill her," I said eventually. "I didn't mean to kill anyone."

"Of course not," he replied.

I wanted to spill my guts to him, tell him everything. How awful it was, how lonely and terrified I was. Everything. It had been so long since I had anyone I could talk to, and I was embarrassingly desperate for real human connection, but now that I had the chance, I found myself unable to speak.

"I think you should go north instead of south," he said eventually. "Not right now, but after the fuss has died down."

"In case you didn't notice," I said, cupping my belly. "I'm kind of on a ticking clock over here."

"I know someone who can help you," he said. "My old friend Harlan Washburn. He's a real radical, anti-government type with no love for any kind of police and his partner Winnie is a midwife. The two of them live in northern Washington and help women escaping domestic violence to cross the border into Canada and start new lives off the grid."

"Off the grid, huh?" I frowned. "I don't know, I'm a city girl. I'm not really the Doomsday Prepper type."

"You are now," he said.

We both drank our tea in silence for several minutes. The cat came over to where I was sitting and head-butted me in the arm, then sat down next to me and started cleaning his big, creamsicle-colored belly like everything was totally normal and nothing bad could possibly happen here. As desperately as I wanted to stay in this safe little bubble of stopped time, I knew that the only reason it had stayed safe was because I hadn't been in it. And the longer I stayed, the less safe it would be.

"Harlan's grandson is in town tomorrow," Wyman said. "He'll take you there."

"I don't have any money," I replied.

"Don't need any," he said. "But I can give you a few bucks to help you on your way."

"I'll pay you back," I said. "Once I get settled."

"Fine, sure," he said, waving away my concern and setting down his now-empty cup. "We can talk more in the morning, but my evening meds make me so tired. Anyway, that couch is pretty comfortable." He handed me a faux fur throw with a cowhide print. "I spend a lot of nights on it myself, when the bedroom seems too lonely. Mitchum will keep you company."

I had a childish urge to ask him to stay until I fell asleep but had to make do with the cat.

I was exhausted but I couldn't sleep. Couldn't get comfortable, couldn't shut off the frantic chatter of my anxious thoughts. I'd drift off for a few minutes and then wake up drowning in sludgy dread and that burnt duct tape smell. My brain kept jabbing me with panicky what-ifs and the Situation kept twisting and kicking me like it was demanding answers. I didn't have any.

Eventually, I got up and wandered into Wyman's studio.

There were crooked stacks of art prints and packing materials piled on every surface and stacked against the walls, but everything seemed dusty and forgotten. Dozens of hard, weathered cowboy faces watched me from every angle as I booted up his computer. None of those faces were Hank's.

I didn't see any files that looked like fake IDs, but I didn't look that hard. I had no reason to believe he would lie to me about getting rid of the one he made for me, I just figured it wouldn't hurt to check. Nothing left but photos and art.

A few of the nested, generically named folders contained erotic images Wyman had sketched out in loving, hyper-realistic detail. Men, naked and fucking in various ways. True to his word, none of them had Hank's face either.

Had Hank ever really existed? Did I make him up? Did I really watch him die or was that another one of my lurid recurring nightmares?

In a strange, cold sweat I scrolled through rugged hands and sunsets and tough squints under shadowy hat brims. Unable to let it go, I must have looked through a hundred files, but no Hank.

I suddenly realized that I couldn't exactly remember what he had looked like. I mean, I had an idea of him, a blocky, broad-shouldered shape cut out of the soft and treacherous tissue of my brain, but what were his eyes like? His mouth? What did he smell like? Taste like? What did his voice sound like when he said my name?

It seemed imperative to remember, but I couldn't.

It was like my former life and everyone in it was burning, hot and toxic as silver nitrate behind me, as I ran towards my uncertain future. Like the past was dissolving, disintegrating and leaving nothing for me to hold onto. It felt hard to breathe, dull pain flaring up in my healing ribs, and I almost scrolled right past him.

But there he was.

Those rough-hewn angles. Pale eyes and broken nose. Regret.

After the Fight was the title of that painting.

But what are you supposed to do after the fight? What happens when you keep on living past The End? What happens when you give it your best shot and still lose and everyone who cares about you dies and you're just hanging around like the one dirty dinner party dish that never got washed. Because that's how I felt, sloppy and gross and reminding everyone of what used to be delicious but has since had all the good parts eaten up and been left out to spoil.

I couldn't look at that painting anymore, so I closed the file and pulled up a browser window. Because I wanted to focus on a man who was still alive and thought about me every day. My new Vukasin. Or, if I was honest, more like I was his.

I rewatched all the videos of Officer William Corbin talking to the press, including a new one where he swore that he would spend the rest of his life working tirelessly to bring me to justice. He'd shorn the wolfman hair down to stubble and it made his pale, sleepless face look fierce and angular, like he just got back from learning kung fu in some secret monastery in Tibet in preparation to clean up the streets. I knew exactly how he felt.

But I also knew that there could be no neat and final resolution for any of us in this strange, recursive revenge trap. The longer I lived, the more people I destroyed. The more people I destroyed, the more people wanted to destroy me. And there was never any winning, never any peace. Because there was no going back to the mythical Before-All-This.

Sure, I'd thought about opting out, about just fucking ending it and being done with this shit. More times that I liked to admit. But I still couldn't bring myself to crash the car while I had an innocent passenger along for the ride. Which is why

Wyman's idea of getting to a place where the Situation could be resolved somehow felt like my only hope.

I crept back to the couch and burrowed under the musty blanket. Mitchum the cat immediately came over and snuggled, purring, against my belly like he was communing with the Situation. I tried to imagine the theoretical sanctuary I was headed to, someplace with a lot of fragrant pine trees and bald eagles and maybe a view of that famous mountain they have up there. Someplace I could feel clean again. Someplace where a child could grow up and learn things that really mattered and have the kind of life where nobody shot at them. With or without me.

It was a nice dream.

14.

It was Wyman's idea to dye my hair. And, yeah sure, I know the chemicals in hair dye are not recommended for people in my situation. But then again, neither is getting shot at.

Wyman had phoned his helper and asked him to pick up a few things for me on the way over, including the hair dye. I wasn't thrilled about roping someone I didn't know into this mess, but Wyman seemed to trust him and it's not like I had any alternatives.

The guy's name was Octavio, mid-thirties maybe with a receding hairline and a strong but heavyset build. He seemed nice, which made me want to urge him to get as far away from me as possible as quickly as possible.

"I got everything you asked for, Mister Earl," he said, handing me a cheap black nylon backpack and a pair of worn brown cowboy boots.

"Thanks," I said, unzipping the bag to check out the contents.

Inside were two chintz church dresses, some drugstore underwear and socks, and a stretchy sports bra. Big, cheap Jackie O sunglasses, a toothbrush and some travel-sized toiletries, along with a box of dye featuring a photo of a smiling model with terrifyingly bright red hair.

"You sure about this?" I said, eyeing the dye box.

"Positive," he said. "People see a redhead, that's what they remember most."

Red would not have been my first choice, and the warm, rusty tone I wound up with was bare-knuckle brawling against my olive complexion in a deeply unflattering way, but it did its job. I didn't look like me at all.

The thrift-store dresses had that weird, dusty mothball scent that made me a little bit nauseous, but I picked the slightly less ugly of the two and put it on anyway. It fit over the Situation just fine, but that was the only nice thing I could say about it.

I never did get those bra pads the lady in the elevator had suggested, so I stuffed some tissues into the sports bra and hoped that the bold, tacky pattern would camouflage the worst of the inevitable stains.

The boots fit fine too, even with how swollen my poor beat-up feet were, but they had that funny feeling of being worn down in the shape of someone else's foot. This whole new version of myself felt that way, like it looked ok from a distance but didn't feel quite right.

The low-rent urban cowgirl getup was topped off with a man's tan suede jacket from the back of Wyman's closet that looked as pristine as the day it was purchased back in 1972.

"Isn't it a bit hot for a jacket?" I asked.

"Not where you're headed," he replied, draping it over my shoulders.

I slipped my arms into the sleeves. It felt heavy and soft and smelled like Bay Rum cologne and cigarettes.

"This belonged to David," he said, smoothing the lapels and smiling. "My…very dear friend. He would have been pleased to have it be included in an exciting adventure like this. He loved crime thrillers."

Wyman's late partner had a first name now, and though Wyman still didn't seem ready to overtly state the true nature of their relationship, I felt secretly glad that he was trusting me this far. After all, I was trusting him with far more dangerous secrets. I hoped my secrets didn't get him killed, like pretty much everyone else who was ever nice to me.

Of course, I didn't realize that there was something else ahead of me in that line.

"Don't forget the new hospice nurse is scheduled to be here at 3:30 today," Octavio said over his shoulder as he carried groceries into the kitchen.

"Oh, don't worry," Wyman said. "We'll still have plenty of time to see Angel on her way."

"Hospice?" I frowned. "What…?"

"Cancer," he said, shrugging. "Very aggressive, they say. What are you gonna do?"

I tried to keep my shit together, but my face must have given me away.

"Oh, it's not so bad," he said. "Bank's gonna take the house. Octavio's gonna take Mitchum." He scratched the cat under his chin. "Not much point hanging around after that, I guess."

I didn't know how to feel about this information, couldn't process it, and at a time when it felt like crying would have been appropriate, tears didn't come.

"I'm so sorry," I managed to say.

Wyman nodded, rummaging in an overstuffed drawer, waving his other hand at me in a dismissive gesture.

"Don't be," he said, taking out a battered leather wallet. "I've made my peace with it. Anyway, I'm happy I could help you and your baby on my way out, Angel."

He handed me a modest handful of twenties.

"Wish it could be more," he said.

"I will pay you back," I said, counting a hundred and forty dollars before slipping the cash into my left sock. "I promise."

"Don't bother," he said. "I don't need it."

15.

"Turn here, Octavio," Wyman said, pointing a knobby finger at a seemingly random spot in the red dirt along the side of the highway.

I could see some tire tracks and a handwritten sign that said "STOCK" with a scratchy arrow pointing down the back side of the fairgrounds, but that was it as far as indications of anything resembling a road. Octavio turned where Wyman had indicated, the little car bouncing across the rocky dirt in a way that made my perpetually full bladder feel like a punching bag.

At the end of that non-road was a cluster of vehicles parked in a somewhat orderly, mutually agreed upon pattern that mimicked a parking lot without the tarmac or markings of any kind. Octavio drove the car to the end of the row and parked next to a large, dented horse trailer emblazoned with the words "Let 'er buck."

When I opened the car door, the smell hit me.

A massive, breathtaking wallop of a smell. Hay and shit and hot, massive animals from some mysterious faraway place and me five years old again back at the Lincoln Park Zoo, equal parts fascinated and terrified.

Octavio had come around to the passenger side to help Wyman, handing him a cane with an ergonomic handle and four rubber feet. Wyman must have noticed my expression of nauseated disgust.

"Breathe it in, city girl," Wyman said with an impish wink. "You're in a whole new world."

I shook my head and slipped on the big sunglasses, tucked

the suede jacket into my backpack and slung it over one shoulder.

We were approached by an odd little vehicle that I could only describe as a monster golf cart. Fat knobby tires, black roll cage and a stubby little truck bed, currently occupied by a very dirty and very happy black-and-white dog. Behind the wheel was an equally dirty and happy human, a tall man with a big grin who looked like he had recently been wearing a hat, but currently wasn't. His sweaty blond hair was flattened to his head in a perfect ring where a hatband would have been.

"Hey, Mister Earl," he said. "Haven't seen you around lately. How you been?"

"Oh, can't complain," Wyman replied, an obvious lie that neither of them seemed to acknowledge. "You seen Wash?"

"He's warming up over by the bucking chutes," the man said. "Too good for the likes of us, as usual." He looked me up and down with a bemused expression. "You taking pictures today?"

"Next time," Wyman said, like there was really gonna be a next time.

The man nodded and drove away, leaving us in a little cloud of dust. His dog watched us from the back of the cart, matted tail wagging and tongue flapping in the breeze.

"You want me to walk with you?" Octavio asked.

"I'm fine," Wyman said, gallantly tucking my hand into his elbow as if he were helping me, not the other way around. "I'll only be a few minutes."

Between the two of us, it was a long, slow walk from the parking area to our destination. Never mind the quick detour to a crooked row of Porta Potties. I had learned the hard way: Never pass up an opportunity for a piss.

The area we entered was located at one end of a large oval

arena surrounded by metal stands. Something was happening in there, I could tell by the clouds of dust and cheers of the crowd, but I couldn't see anything from my vantage point.

What I could see was cowboys.

I'm not just talking about guys with hats, either. I'm talking about full on head-to-toe, chaps and spurs that jingle-jangle-jingle, just-walked-out-of-a-movie fucking cowboys. Some of them had paper numbers pinned to their backs. Some of them had on protective leather vests with high, stiff collars. They wrapped tape around their arms and jostled each other around a bulletin board and huddled over iPhones. They sat on saddles plopped down in the dusty dirt and stretched long fringed legs out with their boots stuck into bulky stirrups. They hung thick ropes from the fences and worked them up and down with wire brushes and rosined gloves. They laughed, prayed and slapped each other's denim asses.

They all seemed to know Wyman.

On the far end was a group of young girls in star-spangled costumes and glittering hats pulling matching socks onto the legs of their restless horses. I'd never been so close to horses in my life, and they seemed so impossibly huge and intimidating with their hard stamping feet and snorting nostrils. It was tough to resist giving them an extra wide berth just to be on the safe side.

"Mister Earl!" the girls called out, waving us over. "Mister Earl! Where's your camera Mister Earl?"

"Next time," he replied. "How's Baylee?"

"Cast comes off next week," one of the girls replied, a tall brunette with the kind of sweet, freckled face you'd see in an ad for organic beauty products.

"Where's Wash at?" Wyman asked.

The girls all looked at me and my belly for an uncomfortably long moment, exchanging smirking side-eyes and then burst into giggles.

"Over there," the tall brunette said, tipping her chin toward a solitary figure with earbuds in and hat brim pulled down low, performing a series of what looked like dance steps. Planting one foot firmly in the dust and then pivoting away over and over. Lost in his own world.

He was wearing the same dirty straw hat as the other cowboys, but his bulkier, almost ballistic looking vest was composed of two stiff, scuffed-up polymer plates like a turtle's shell with velcro straps down the sides of his body, and he wore it over a sweat-damp white undershirt instead of a long-sleeved western shirt. Everything else was different too. Loose black board shorts instead of jeans and chaps. Neon green and orange cleats instead of boots. Elaborate metal brace on one scarred knee. He didn't notice us until we were right behind him.

When he turned to face us, pulling out one earbud, I saw that he was wearing clown makeup.

I didn't say *you've got to be fucking kidding me* out loud, but I thought it so hard I was sure Wyman must have psychically heard me. This was the guy who was gonna save my ass? Bozo the Cowboy?

Ok, to be fair, it wasn't like he was in full greasepaint with a ball on his nose and a lurid John Wayne Gacy smile. He just had these sharp white shapes like abstract lightning zig-zagging across his high, wide cheekbones and hooking around his dark eyes. The tip of his small but broad nose was painted red and there was a thin black cross penciled on his chin. His dark eyes lit up when he saw us, and he flashed a friendly and genuine grin that made me feel like a terrible person for my previous, uncharitable thoughts. He was missing a front tooth.

"Well, hey there, Mister Earl," he said, grabbing an oversized and eye-wateringly loud Hawaiian shirt that had been draped over the metal fence beside him and slipping it on over his vest. "Who's your friend?"

"This is An…" Wyman began, but I cut him off before he could finish saying Angel.

"…gie," I said instead, sticking out my hand. "Angie."

He took his hat off, because of course he did, and then shook my hand. His dark hair beneath the hat was buzzed short and already receding into a deep V even though he couldn't have been older than 25. His hand was hard and calloused and reminded me of Hank's.

"Guilford Washburn," he said. "But my friends call me Wash."

"Listen, Wash," Wyman said, dropping his voice and taking a step closer. "Angie here is in trouble." He put a hand on my belly. "Life or death type trouble. Can you take her to Harlan?"

"Course I can," Wash said instantly, his painted face gone grave and serious. "You bet. I'm fighting bulls in Ada again this year, so we'd have to hit that first but after that, no problem."

Something about that moment really stuck with me. The way it didn't even seem open for debate. I thought about times in my life where I'd been called on to help someone and hesitated or had to mull it over. This total stranger in the silly clown makeup didn't hesitate for a second. Like it never would have occurred to him to say no.

I didn't deserve that kid. Or more importantly, he didn't deserve me.

"Find you a shady place to sit," Wash said. "And I'll be back in a minute, ok?"

It struck me then that he didn't have the kind of strong accent I would have expected from someone like him, all broad, twangy Texas vowels or maybe a warm Southeast drawl like Hank's. His voice was gentle and deep with what sounded to my ears like an unremarkable, neutral American accent, but yet still peppered with a distinct kind of cowboy syntax I couldn't quite put my finger on.

"Ok," I said, not knowing what else to say.

There was a huge storm front of living noise rolling towards us, hoofs and snorts and bellows and harsh, metallic crashes and suddenly the fence behind Wash was all that stood between us and a raging river of hulking, multicolored bulls. I took an involuntary step back, hands over my belly and Wash chuckled, putting his hat back on his head.

"Don't worry, Angie," he said. "You're safe here."

"You're in good hands," Wyman said, patting my arm.

I wished I believed that.

16.

I walked Wyman back to his car, hugged his frail little body tight and managed to hold it together until Octavio drove away before disintegrating into a blubbering and hysterical mess. It was like watching your safe, familiar spaceship fly away, leaving you marooned on an alien planet.

I eventually pulled myself together, hit the Porta Potty again, and then headed over to find someplace to get off my swollen feet. There were a few small groups sitting together on coolers or in folding chairs, but one group of three blondes without hats seemed the least alien and the most approachable.

They were in their early to mid-twenties, sitting on a low concrete wall drinking brightly colored Mexican soft drinks in glass bottles. All unnaturally curvy and bottom-heavy with sculpted wasp waists. They looked like they were on a porn set, waiting to shoot their scene for COCK-HUNGRY COWGIRLS 3. Tiny, cut-off denim shorts. Sparkly, slashed up t-shirts that revealed more than they covered. Long, jeweled nails. Full makeup despite the heat. My kinda girls.

"Got a spare pop?" I asked. "I think I'm melting."

"Sure," said the one on the right, a hard-faced platinum blonde with a full sleeve of beautiful scrollwork tattoos. She reached into a small Styrofoam cooler and pulled out a pineapple-flavored drink, popping off the lid with a bottle opener on her keychain and handing it to me. "Who are you with?"

"Um...Wash," I said before taking a huge swig from the icy bottle. It was the best drink I'd ever had.

The girls exchanged loaded glances and then the darker

golden blonde on the left smiled and patted the wall beside her. I lowered my bulk slowly down to sit and tucked my backpack between my feet.

"Oh honey," she said. "I know sayin' this now is like closing the barn door after the horses are out, but you are *so* on the wrong end of the arena."

The girl in the middle, a strawberry blonde with blinding white veneers in a sly, mischievous grin leaned in to speak in a confidential stage-whisper.

"Fuck all the roughies you like," she said. "But you want to marry a timey."

The three blondes laughed. Not squeaky schoolgirl giggles like the star-spangled cowgirls, more like the kind of full-throated, bawdy bar laughter that made me feel included, not excluded. I couldn't help but laugh a little too, mostly at my own expense.

"I'm from Chicago," I said. "I don't have the slightest fucking idea what any of that even means."

"Don't pay Lindy no mind," the platinum blonde said, clinking her bottle against mine. "Wash is a good one."

"Not bad for a clown, huh?" I joked.

"Don't let him hear you call him that," the strawberry blonde said. "Or you gonna end up a single mother."

I was about to explain that I just met Wash and that he wasn't responsible for the Situation, when the golden blonde arched a heavily penciled cartoon eyebrow and said:

"Speak of the devil."

"Hey, Wash," the three of them drawled in unison, stretching out his name like bubblegum.

He had put on a pair of comically enormous and ragged cut-off jeans with red suspenders over his other shorts. Really it was less like a practical garment and more he was wearing a denim sandwich board over his crotch. The denim had various patches sewn on all over, logos for companies that made things like farm equipment, whiskey and boots. There were three mismatched bandanas tied and hanging from the belt loops, one on either side and one in back, like a hanky code for someone who couldn't make up their mind about what they were into. He also had an American flag bandana tied around his dusty neck.

"Ladies," he said to the blondes. He nodded but didn't take his hat off. "I got you a seat in the stands, Angie, if you want to watch the perf."

"Ok," I said. I was saying that a lot these days. I struggled to my feet and turned back to the blondes. "Thanks for the drink."

"See you on down the trail, Chicago!" the platinum blonde said, saluting me with her bottle.

As soon as we were out of earshot, Wash tipped his head towards mine.

"You don't want to be hanging around them bunnies," he said.

"Bunnies?" I repeated.

"Buckle bunnies," he said. "Certain ladies that just want to... Well, you know."

His expression was so sincere, it took everything I had in me not to laugh out loud. I didn't have the heart to tell him that I was one of those certain ladies too. And then some. I changed the subject.

"Right, ok," I said as he led me around to a side gate that opened into the stands. "So exactly what do you do here? I was told I shouldn't call you a clown or you'll get mad."

"I ain't no entertainer," he said with an indulgent smile. "I'm a bullfighter."

"Like a matador?" I mimed waving a cape. "*Olé* and all that?"

I felt a wave of sudden nausea. I didn't know if I had the stomach to watch a bloody bullfight but couldn't figure out how to gracefully get out of it without offending my new grease-paint guardian.

"Nah," he said. "Nothing like that. You'll see."

He moved a stack of flyers for something called Cowboy Church down to the end of the lowest row of seats and directed me to sit in their place, calling a young girl over to give me a bottle of water, even though I hadn't finished my pop yet.

"Keep an eye on her for me," he told the girl.

A booming announcer's voice filled the arena, drowning out the girl's response.

"Ladies and gentlemen, are y'all ready for some bull riding?"

The crowd cheered, and to my surprise Wash jumped right over the fence and down into the dirt arena below.

"Give it up for your bullfighters, those brave men who put it all on the line to protect our cowboys, Guilford Washburn and Colt McKee!"

Wash touched the brim of his hat and then pointed up at the sky as he was joined out on the dirt by a second man. The other guy was inexplicably wearing a completely different outfit and no paint on his ruddy face. Instead of the baggy, colorful clown clothes, this guy was dressed more like a soccer player in matching red and yellow shorts and jersey with black socks and cleats. His jersey had logo patches all over it and his last name spelled out across the back. The only thing that was the same was their battered straw cowboy hats and the shape of the bulky protective vest beneath their shirts. They high-fived each other and then motioned for the audience to cheer.

"And the Man in the Can," the announcer said. "Cal Overland!"

The back gate opened and out came a guy dressed more like

Wash, rolling a big, duct-tape-covered barrel. I felt more confused than ever.

I won't bore you with all the details of the rodeo. Either you already know what it's like and you don't need my clueless, city girl play-by-play or else you don't know what it's like and don't really care. I'll just tell you this. It turned out that Wash's job wasn't to "fight" the bulls like I had imagined. It was to get them to chase him instead of the poor sap that just fell or jumped off their back. Whether they made the eight seconds or not, Wash was there beside them, ready and willing to get clobbered by a giant, pissed off animal while the rider got to safety.

At one point one of the bull riders got stuck somehow, unable to let go of the rope and flopping around like a cat toy as his bull continued to spin and buck. Wash had to jump up on the bull's back and cut the guy loose. All in all, it was pretty impressive, though I could see his knee was bothering him, the one with the metal brace.

I wouldn't do his job for all the money in the world. That being said, he probably wouldn't do mine either.

Once all that was over and the fans started filing out of the arena, Wash came back over to where I was sitting.

"How'd you like it?" he asked with a crooked grin.

"You were amazing," I said. "But it's not like I'm a good judge of that kind of thing. After all, this actually is my first rodeo."

"Is that right?" His affable grin grew wider. He seemed utterly unselfconscious about that missing tooth. "Don't worry, we'll break you in easy."

I would have taken that as some kind of lewd innuendo, but somehow it just didn't feel that way. He took my hand and helped me to my feet, walking me back through the gate in the stands and behind the chutes.

"Normally we'd stick around for the fireworks," he said as we cut through the little backstage enclosure and into the parking area. "But I need to get on the road to make Ada."

"Ok," I said, not wanting to tell him how much I hated fireworks anyway. If I never heard that sound again it would be too fucking soon.

He led me over to a scuffed-up midnight-blue pickup truck that was probably older than he was and opened the passenger door.

"Lemme get the air on for you," he said, reaching across my belly to key the ignition and cranking the AC. "And I'll get cleaned up real quick."

"Great," I said. "Thanks."

I sat alone for a little while in the truck, watching through the bug-splattered windshield as cowboys and bunnies paired up and took off, wondering what I was getting myself into. The interior of the cab was dusty but uncluttered, except for a plastic go-cup from a fried chicken place I'd never heard of that was about a third full of some vile, dark liquid that I couldn't even look at without feeling a swell of nausea in the back of my throat.

I immediately realized what it was when Wash got into the driver's seat, lifted it to his lips and spat into it, then set it back in the cup holder. He took off his hat and set it on the dash, and I could see a distinct bulge in his cheek. The greasepaint had been scrubbed off his broad, tan face and he looked much younger and lankier without his protective vest under his clean t-shirt. Without his hat on, he looked pretty much like a million other ordinary guys his age.

"You ready to hit the road?" he asked.

"Sure," I said.

"How about some music?"

He set his iPhone into a dash-mounted holder and keyed up some tunes while pulling out of the lot in a wide fan of dust. Angry hip-hop blared from the speakers, and I guess he could tell I was shocked by his selection because he flashed his missing tooth in that crooked half smile.

"You expecting Hank Williams or something?" he asked.

"I guess I was," I admitted.

"Well, you got a few things left to learn, don't you?"

17.

"So, you're from Chicago?"

We'd been on the road for several hours and the sun was sulking on the western horizon behind us. My back and hips hurt, and I pretty much always had to pee, but I didn't complain. The vibration of the road seemed to have lulled the Situation into hibernation.

"Yeah," I said. "Most of my family lives north of Roosevelt, but I grew up in Bridgeport."

As soon as it was out of my mouth, I realized that I should have lied. Being tired and sore was no excuse, and if I didn't start tightening up my backstory, I was gonna have some serious problems. All I could do is hope that a guy like him wouldn't know Bridgeport from Lakeview.

"That right?" he said, pausing to spit into the gross cup. "Must have been rough, on account of all them murders and crimes."

I had to stifle a relieved laugh, imagining the old Lithuanian lady who ran the bakery next door conking twelve-year-old me over the head with a loaf of sourdough rye and taking my Spider Woman wallet. It was way better for both of us if he thought of Chicago as an undifferentiated hellscape of urban decay and gang violence.

"You have no idea," I replied, letting him think I was agreeing before deflecting back to him. "How about you?"

"Omak," he replied. "That's in the state of Washington. Mama was a barrel racer, so I grew up on the trail. She put me on a sheep as soon as I could stand up. Got herself killed in a wreck when I was seventeen and that's when I decided to stop riding bulls and start fighting 'em."

"Why do they call what you do bullfighting," I asked. "When it's really more like bull distracting or bull avoiding."

"Dunno," he said. "It's just what they call it. It's not like we don't have moves in common with the Spanish boys. We're just way tougher than they are."

"How's that?"

"Because we don't kill our bulls. They live and learn the fakes, learn to watch our feet. Our bulls have got your number."

"So why do you do it?" I asked. "For the adrenaline?"

"I mean, yeah, pretty much." He spat into the cup. "Anyone who tells you different is either lying to you or to themselves. We dress it up in hero clothing same as firefighters and SWAT guys and anybody else who runs towards danger instead of away from it, but with freestyle you don't have to bother with any of that. There's nobody to save. It's just you and the bull."

"Considering the fact that you were willing to help someone like me, despite there being a zillion sensible reasons not to," I said. "I think maybe there's a little more hero in you than you let on."

He shrugged, grinned.

"Maybe so."

We drove in silence for a few minutes before he spoke again.

"We can talk about it, if you want to," he said, gesturing to the Situation with his eyes still on the road.

I got hit with a sudden spiraling sense of time folding in on itself, repeating like two mirrors facing each other in some ritzy club in Vegas. I saw a different version of myself in a different car with a different man who also wanted to help me. A dead man. I felt trapped between a past I couldn't forget and a future I couldn't imagine.

"Maybe later," I said.

We drove. Didn't speak.

"You got a girlfriend?" I finally asked, deflecting again.

"Yeah. Well, not really a girlfriend, but…"

We drove. I didn't say anything.

"She's a redhead, like you." I almost laughed but managed not to. So that was the real reason Wyman had suggested I go red. "I always did have a thing for redheads, and this one, she's real special, but…"

More silence. Then:

"She's married."

What was I supposed to say to that? I didn't exactly have a moral high ground from which to scold him about the evils of infidelity.

"I ain't a bad person," he said.

"I think I'd agree with that assessment of your character."

A little rind of a smile lingered for a moment in the corner of his mouth.

"That's only on account of the fact that you don't know me so well."

There was really only one bad person in this car, and there was no way he was gonna win that particular dick measuring contest with someone like me, so I just kept quiet.

His smile faded, his expression gone stormy and troubled.

"I know it's a sin, what she wants, but…"

More silence. The road unspooled. Eighteen-wheelers lumbered past.

"She's the one. You know? I can't live without her."

I was not expecting things to get this heavy this quickly. I let more silence stretch between us.

"Do you mind if we make another stop?" I asked. "I gotta pee again."

"Sure thing."

*

The gas station was basically every nowheresville gas station you've ever been to. Pumps. Combo convenience store and burger/pizza/coffee joint off to one side. Parking lot, nowhere near full. The only thing that was unique was a strange little cluster of amoeba-like metal shapes over by the far end of the lot. Art, maybe? But why? Why here?

It wasn't until later that I noticed there was no security camera. Not outside, anyway.

I used the grim little bathroom around the side of the building and then went into the store looking for Wash but had to leave again almost immediately. The school-lunch smell of cheap, microwaved pizza and old hot dog water mixed with industrial floor cleaner instantly turned my stomach. I'd never been this sensitive to smells in the past, so I figured it must have something to do with the Situation.

As I fast-waddled towards the door, I nearly ran into a guy coming in. An older guy with a clean straw cowboy hat and hazel eyes behind spidery steel glasses. He had a weak chin and a loose, wattled neck buttoned into a too-tight collar. Same dusty Wrangler jeans as everybody in this part of the world, apparently, but paired with perfectly white, fresh-out-of-the-box sneakers instead of boots. My eyes were fixed on the odd shoes, shoes that seemed so out of character, like there'd been a mistake in the wardrobe department, when he said:

"Ma'am."

I looked up and he was touching the brim of his hat and holding the door for me, and he fucking knew me.

18.

I ducked my head like that would help somehow and pushed past him, desperate to be outside and feeling frantic, panicky.

Outside wasn't any better. There was no one else around. Just a few empty cars. Wash had taken the keys to his truck with him so it's not like I could take off without him even if I wanted to. There was nowhere to run to on foot, but my mind was all over the place, looking for some way to get away from that knowing smirk.

I stood over by the weird sculptures, breathing exhaust fumes and the smell of my own panic sweat. Where the fuck was Wash? What was taking him so fucking long? I was starting to seriously consider just running out to the highway and trying to flag down a passing car when I was hit by a powerful, irrational fear of being alone.

I have no idea where that came from. I always used to describe my personality type as a "slutty loner." Plenty of friends, many with benefits, but always alone at the end of the night. Alone was my jam, my default setting, but my treacherous and fickle body was clearly using the Situation to hijack everything I thought I knew about myself.

I had my eyes squeezed shut for just a second and when I opened them again, I wasn't alone anymore.

The guy who knew me was right beside me.

"Angel Dare," he said. "As I live and breathe."

For a second, we both just stood there. Wind whipped my damaged, coppery hair into my face, but his hat stayed on like it was nailed on. I was trying to make my lips move, to formulate some kind of denial, anything at all, but my thoughts were a scattered jumble, and nothing came out.

He smiled and reached into an inner pocket, and I figured he's gonna shoot me right here in this shitty gas station and hey, at least I won't have to worry about the Situation anymore.

He didn't shoot me. He pulled out a badge. A fucking cop, but that made me feel worse, not better.

His smile grew, wide and cruel. I was pretty sure his perfect teeth were fake.

"I love your movies," he said, tucking the badge back into the pocket it came from.

So, it was like that. Fine. Nothing I couldn't handle.

I knelt on the rough, gritty ground in front of his incongruous white sneakers, steeling myself for what needed to be done and hoping he'd be quick about it. The last thing I needed was to have to explain to Wash why I was blowing somebody's grandpa in the parking lot. The guy had on way too much cologne and tasted bitter and soapy like maybe he'd sprayed the stuff directly on his otherwise unremarkable junk. Which, honestly, I'll take over the other end of the hygiene spectrum any day of the week. I was able to finish him swiftly with minimal effort.

I spat into the dirt and was wiping my mouth on the back of my hand when he grabbed my hair and tipped my face up.

"Nice work," he said, tucking everything back into his jeans and giving my face a condescending, playful little slap. "I'm still gonna have to take you in though, on account of being a friend of Corbin. No hard feelings."

I flashed back hard to the last guy who slapped my face like that and felt my body flush all over with the heat of incandescent rage as he hauled me awkwardly up to my feet by my hair.

"Get the fuck off me," I said.

I'd like to tell you that I said it in a powerful, badass, action dialog kind of way but it came out more like a half-choked squeak.

I was twisting and flailing wildly, arms windmilling, and eyes squeezed shut so I didn't see Wash until he was pulling the guy off of me.

When I looked up, I saw the two of them locked in a tight and dirty barroom clinch. The older guy's hat had finally been knocked off and was sitting on its crown in the dust near my feet, but somehow, miraculously, Wash's was still on his head.

They swung hard to the left and it looked like Wash's leg hit the rippled metal edge of one of the amoeba sculptures.

He let out a sharp, stifled grunt and staggered backwards, clutching his bad knee. His face was bright red, eyes narrowed down to slits. The older guy took this opportunity to take a big swing.

Even through his pain, Wash could clearly see the punch coming from way back because he slipped fluidly to one side like he was dodging a bull and then used the guy's pissed-off momentum to body slam him into the sculpture.

The guy swore and dropped to a knee in the dirt, clutching a bleeding nose but I barely noticed because all I could see was his badge, which had just fallen out of his pocket and landed face up on the ground beside him.

I couldn't let Wash know this guy was a cop. There would be no way someone like Wash would still help me if he knew I was a criminal on the lam from the police. My mind was in a frantic whirl trying to cook up some kind of explanation. Maybe my abusive ex was a cop? Maybe that guy was one of his buddies on the force who was trying to…what? I couldn't say arrest me. Kidnap me?

Then he spoke up.

"Why the hell are you protecting this whore, son? I mean…"

Well, that's it, I thought. *It's all coming out now.*

But I never found out what he was going to say because Wash punched him, then grabbed him and smashed his face into the now bloody metal amoeba. I took that opportunity to casually put my foot down over his badge.

"You ok, Angie?" Wash asked.

"Just give me a minute," I said, sliding the badge under my foot towards one of the other amoebas and clutching the sculpture's edge. "I think I'm gonna throw up again."

He nodded and politely turned his back, limping away to give me some privacy.

The second he turned away I used my foot to shove the badge under the base of the sculpture. Then I looked down at the cop. He wasn't 100% knocked out, but close enough.

They say the more people you kill, the easier it gets. I don't know about that, but I certainly wasn't sorry to see this fucker go.

It was a huge risk. Wash was a good five yards away now, but he could turn around at any moment and catch me in the act. But it was an even bigger risk to leave this guy alive. Because if I did, then Wash would be wanted too. An accessory to my growing list of crimes. I couldn't let that happen.

I didn't let myself think about what a bad idea that might be, I just started making loud retching noises. Using the noise as cover, I knelt with my by now quite considerable weight on the chest of the semi-conscious cop, watching Wash's silhouette against the gas station lights as I pinched the cop's nose closed with one hand while covering his mouth with the other. I added a shin on his neck just to speed things up a bit, all while keeping up with the puke noises to cover the sound of the scuffle. The Situation started slam-dancing inside my belly. Was it agitated by all the adrenaline coursing through my system or was it trying to help? Can you be an accessory to murder before you're even born?

I had a pretty hairy moment where I was sure the gig was up. The cop's eyes had gone wide and wild, not totally aware but seeming to grasp what was happening on some deep animal level, and his body started whipping from side to side against me like a trapped snake.

"Angie?" Wash called from where he was standing with his head still thankfully averted.

I let out an extra loud retching sound and then spit off to one side of the cop's head.

"I'm fine," I said. "Just…"

Again, I let loose with the dramatic noises, all the while leaning harder on the cop's wattled neck. He'd stopped moving by then, but I wasn't taking any chances.

When I was sure that he was done moving for good, I struggled to my feet and pretended to kick dirt over puke that didn't exist. Funny how, once you accept that you're a bad person, doing bad shit gets so much easier.

I hustled over to Wash and took his arm, leaning heavily against him. My whole body felt weak and limp, like I might pass out now that all that mama bear energy had drained away.

"Let's get the hell out of here," I said.

Wash walked me over to the passenger side of the truck and opened the door. I'd just killed a man with my bare hands, but I still needed an embarrassing amount of help getting my bulky ass up into the cab. I think he probably noticed that I pissed myself a little while I was killing that guy, but he was nice enough not to mention it.

When I finally got myself stuffed into the passenger seat, I felt a massive, irrational wave of emotion and threw my arms around Wash, ugly crying noisily against his clean-smelling shirt.

"Hey now," he said, patting my back gently like I was a child. "You're alright. That sumbitch ain't gonna hurt you no more. You want me to go get you some water?"

I did, desperately, but I shook my head no. What I really wanted was to get the fuck away from the body of the man I just murdered. I could still see his stupid white sneakers sticking out from behind the sculptures on the far side of the parking lot.

A young Mexican couple came out of the rest stop doors, chatting happily and sharing a slurpee. They didn't seem to notice the white shoes, but that could change at any moment as they strolled across the lot towards their parked car.

"Let's go," I said.

"Ok, then," Wash said. "Watch your feet."

I gave a small, sheepish smile and pulled my feet into the cab. He closed the door and went around to the driver's side.

We got the hell out of there.

19.

"What the hell was that about anyway?" he asked. "Do you know that guy?"

I couldn't keep deflecting forever. I had to say something. Wash was a good kid, but he wasn't stupid. I felt like I owed him some kind of explanation, even if it wasn't the truth. Though to be honest, I was losing track of what was or wasn't true myself.

"He's a friend of my ex," I said. "The abusive ex that's been trying to find me, to convince me to get back together with him. That creep didn't even want the baby at first." It felt weird saying the word *baby* out loud after avoiding it for so long. "He beat the shit out of me when he first found out and told me to get rid of it, but now he's changed his mind. He's been having me followed."

"That ain't right," Wash said with such earnest intensity that I knew I'd hit a nerve. I felt like a total monster. "Putting hands on a woman for any reason, especially one in your delicate condition, is about the lowest a man can go."

I suddenly felt a wave of real nausea hit the back of my throat.

"Pull over," I said through gritted teeth.

"Are you ok?" he asked.

"Fucking pull over!"

He did, and I tumbled out onto the shoulder like a chubby sea lion being rolled off her iceberg by a killer whale. Unfortunately, nobody showed up to eat me.

Throwing up and crying at the same time is surprisingly difficult, but I was getting used to it. I was getting used to all kinds of deeply unpleasant things.

Wash got out and stood at a discrete distance, facing away with his hatless head turned up to the night sky as if the answer was up there somewhere. The sky looked fake, like CGI. Too many stars out here. Wherever the fuck here was.

He gave me a minute to crawl a little way away from my puke and get whatever shit I had left together before easing over, slow and sideways like I was a nervous animal.

"Hey," he said. "You ok?"

He held out a hand. I nodded and took it and let him help me to my feet.

What he did next was so unexpected that it took me a second to realize that he wasn't trying to feel me up. I probably would have been less shocked if he had been.

He put his hands on my belly and started praying.

My face went hot, my body hunched and awkward. I didn't know what I was supposed to do with my own arms so they just kind of hovered halfway up and out like frozen jazz hands. Amazingly, I did not burst into flames or anything.

"Lord Jesus," he said. "We just praise your name and thank you for your wise and guiding hand, for keeping Angie and her precious baby from harm and giving me the strength to protect and help them along the way. We pray that you continue to watch over them and bless them on their journey."

"Amen," he said, looking earnestly into my face until I felt compelled to say it too.

"Amen," I echoed, crossing myself like I hadn't done since Catholic school.

I just assumed that's what you were supposed to do at the end of a prayer, but I guess not, because he didn't cross himself. I turned away, chewing my lower lip and looking up at the too-starry sky. It was starting to feel cold, or maybe it was just me.

"Here," he said.

I turned back and he had taken off a necklace and was putting it over my head. It was a beaded leather cross with a raw chunk of turquoise in the center.

"My mama made this," he said. "It always brought me luck. I reckon you and that little one need it way more than I do."

"Thanks," I said. He had no idea how bad my luck really was. "I don't know if you were planning to drive all night or what. But I could really use a shower."

What I really needed was to change my damp and rancid underwear, but I didn't tell him that.

"Well, normally I just pull over and catch forty in the truck bed," he said. "But I ain't never had a lady in your condition along for the ride, so I guess we could stop at a motel for a few hours."

I guess I was hoping for some kind of cool quirky vintage joint with a big neon sign featuring a waving cowgirl, but we wound up at a Days Inn. Our beige, bland, forgettable room was indistinguishable from every other hotel I'd occupied over the past six months. It smelled like industrial air freshener and forgotten coats that sat too long in the lost-and-found box.

The room also had two beds. Wash had been all ready to be a gentleman and spring for separate rooms, but I got embarrassingly panicky about the idea of being alone. I let him think I needed his protection to feel safe, which wasn't entirely untrue. But it was also like my body was betraying me by issuing its own demands. In the same way that some people in my situation crave pickles, I craved the presence of other humans like I never had before. It certainly wasn't a sex thing. It was something much more primal.

When I got out of the claustrophobic coffin of a shower and into the other ugly dress from my backpack, I could hear Wash on the phone. I had no idea who he was talking to, but the intense tone of his voice made me think this had to be the married girlfriend. I could only catch snippets of his near-whispered conversation.

"...you know I do."

"...it's just that..."

"...c'mon now, don't..."

"This ain't right. You know it ain't." Then the door to the room opened and shut. When I came out of the steamy bathroom, I could see that he had taken the conversation outside. There was a part of me that was convinced that he had driven away and abandoned me, which was utterly ridiculous, but I still teetered on the edge of tears until he came back in.

I was really over this fucking Situation.

20.

We both slept until the sun came up. Him like a log, on his back with his body perfectly straight, hands folded on his chest like a funeral parlor corpse. Me lightly if at all and as curled up as I could be, first on one side then the other, clutching and shoving away various pillows as I struggled to find a semi-comfortable position. I couldn't shut my brain off.

Eventually I gave up and wandered down to the cramped and outdated business center. There was only one computer, older than dirt and excruciatingly slow, but nobody else was on it so I was able to surreptitiously check up on the latest details about my case.

It seemed like the frenzy around me was tapering off a little. Not gone, just slipping off the top of the outrage charts in the perpetually scandalous City of Angels. I'd been usurped by a viral cell phone video in which a reality star went on an unhinged racist rant after throwing kombucha at her stylist in Trashy Lingerie. There was nothing anywhere about the dead guy at the rest stop.

Corbin had a few new interviews, but they were for lesser-known news organizations, one that seemed like some kind of cop groupie website and another that was hyperlocal to the city where he lived. He was saying all the same shit about me, but with more intensity, more desperation. I wondered who was taking care of the baby.

I didn't know what time Wash wanted to get back on the road, so I didn't know when to wake him up. When I got back into the room around 6AM, he was already up and agitated, worrying that we were running late.

"Better leadfoot it from here on out," he said, putting his hat on his head and grabbing my backpack together with his duffel bag. "Do you mind if we just go through the drive through?"

I didn't mind. I was used to eating fast food fries in the car and besides, it would allow me to avoid drawing attention to the fact that I was feeling intensely anxious and paranoid about going into rest stops after what had happened at the last one.

We talked about inconsequential things. Anything but the Situation. He didn't seem to want to talk about the married girlfriend either, so we talked about movies and music and other ephemera. We talked about Washington State and about freestyle bullfighting, which apparently didn't involve any riders and mostly just seemed to be a way to showcase various moves like jumps and fakes. He told me about his plan to open a bullfighting school back in Omak when he retired, which he figured would be in another five years or so. He said he figured there was no point wasting money to get his missing tooth fixed until then, since he'd probably bust up the new grill just as soon as it was set.

Any time he asked about me, I just deflected back to him like a therapist.

"Tell me about your grandfather," I said.

"Harlan?" He sighed. "He's a character, that's for sure."

"How do you mean?"

"Well, he's an atheist and ain't afraid to tell you all about how wrong everyone is but him. He's also pretty much against any kind of government. Believes the whole thing was invented to steal land from Indigenous people and make us all weak and dependent on supermarkets and foreign gasoline and all that."

"He's Native American?"

"Nah," he said. "But my grandma's side of the family is Methow. My mama wouldn't speak to him all through my childhood, on account of the fact that he took up with her mama's sister before she was even in the ground."

"Is that Winnie?" I asked. "The midwife?"

"That's the one," he said. "Auntie Win ain't a bad person, don't get me wrong, and she's some kinda saint for putting up with him, Lord knows, but I never really got to know her until after my mama was gone. She's all about helping babies and their mamas, so you'll be in good hands."

I nodded, mind wandering again to this elusive fantasy landscape of piney green mountains and deep, cold rivers and a different kind of life, one that couldn't be farther removed from the smoggy suburban sprawl of Porn Valley, Los Angeles. I knew what I was doing was more than a little crazy, that the chances of this all adding up to happily ever after for someone like me were slim, but I didn't have anything else to keep me going.

Hours passed and the scenery fluctuated between beautiful and boring and back again and before I knew it, we were in Oklahoma. When we got out to stretch, I noticed him favoring his bad knee more than ever.

"How's your knee?" I asked when we got back in the car. "Does it hurt?"

"Nah," he said, lifting that gross cup to his lips to spit into it. "Got my ear tore half off by a bull rope once. That hurt."

"Wow," I said, wishing that I could have come up with something less lame to say instead.

I really wanted to say, *Why the hell are you helping me?*

I didn't.

"They were able to sew it back on, huh?" I said instead. Not much better, but it was all I could come up with.

"Yep," he said, touching the top rim of his right ear. "Good as new."

We drove in silence. He watched the road. I stared at his ear. It was slightly crooked and had a thick white c-shaped scar curving around behind it. In spite of all that, it was a pretty decent looking ear. Not all fucked up like some of the fighters' ears I'd seen. Not like Hank's ears.

"Your knee is going to be ok for this contest thing you're doing, right?" I asked before I could stop myself.

There was a long pause. Another spit.

"Don't take this the wrong way, Angie," he finally said. "But we're about an hour outside of Ada and I need to start getting my head right. I don't normally talk before a big freestyle fight. It's just how I do things."

"Sorry," I said.

"It's ok," he said, like he was the one imposing on me, not the other way around. "Find you some music."

21.

There was already a crowd in front of the arena. We didn't pull into the jammed parking lot, opting instead to drive around to one side where a guy in a broke-brim ball cap waved us through an open gate.

There was an elaborate system of thick metal fence pieces that had been hooked together to form a wide, closed-in walkway between what looked like large animal holding pens and a massive, industrial-sized roll-up door. The pens were blocked from my current view, but I could hear and smell the presence of hostile bovines.

When Wash parked the truck, we were immediately approached by two men in what I was starting to recognize as bullfighter attire. One younger and dressed in the modern jersey-and-shorts style I'd seen back in Arizona and one older and sporting a more traditional costume, like Wash.

The younger one was blond and square-jawed under the same brand of natural straw cowboy hat that Wash had on. He had an old-fashioned, Flash Gordon kind of face. Faded chambray eyes set a little too close together and a scruff of reddish stubble on his big cleft chin. No greasepaint. His build was bulked up in the torso by that stiff protective vest, but his arms and legs were long and lean. He was a good six inches taller than his older buddy.

The older one was shorter, softer in the middle and not what anybody would call handsome. A big bulky nose that seemed permanently reddened from too much time in the sun, or in bars, or possibly both. A thick, dark brown beard and an actual and apparently unironic waxed mustache. His white greasepaint zig zags were thinner and sharper than Wash's. No cross design anywhere. His hat was black felt, and his narrow gray eyes were sharp, clever and looking for trouble.

"Late again," the blond said as Wash got out from behind the wheel and stuck his hat on his head.

"About eight months late by the look of it," the older one said, eyeing my belly with a mischievous smirk as he reached out a hand to help me down from the truck.

"This here is Angie," Wash said. "Get her a seat, willya?"

He leaned close to the blond, cutting his eyes towards the older man.

"And keep her away from Chase."

The accused put his hand to his chest and staggered as if he'd been shot as Wash started walking away.

"Now that's just mean," he called after Wash, voice full of faux hurt. Here was the kind of juicy, full-tilt Texas accent I'd expected to hear more of when I first arrived. "Cruel and unusual defamation of my character, which I will have you know is as pure and clean as your late mama's pussy."

I snorted back a helpless half laugh and Chase turned to me with a surprised grin, the charm turned up to eleven.

"Tell me, darlin'," he said. "What's an earthy and knowing red-headed woman of the world such as yourself doing with a dickless boy scout like Wash?"

The blond took my arm, deliberately sliding his body in between Chase and me and turning me fluidly away like a ballroom dancer leading a less experienced partner.

"Don't pay him no mind," the blond said. "He's harmless."

It suddenly occurred to me that I should have wished Wash good luck or hugged him or something. I looked back over my shoulder and saw him walking in the other direction. I could tell his knee was still bothering him, but he was trying not to let it show. He was in his own world, lost to me.

The blond led me to that large roll-up door leading into the back side of the arena. There was an older guy with no hat sitting on a folding chair, reading a deeply foxed paperback novel that looked like it had lived a long hard life before it found its way into his hands.

"Hey, Sage," the guy said, eying my belly. "Ma'am."

"Don't look at me," the blond said with a big white smile. "She's with Wash."

"Wash?" The guy raised his eyebrows, seeming both surprised and impressed. "Well, ok then."

I was about to explain that the Situation was a pre-existing condition that had nothing to do with Wash, but I never got the chance.

Funny, how deep in you can get just by not saying no.

Inside the building, there was a maze of modular fencing set up in multiple sections with a long corridor leading to what had to be the actual arena itself. Tarps had been hung to block sightlines in certain segments of the maze, but I could hear and smell bulls, stomping and snorting on the other side of the plastic cloth. There were stiff protective vests and several pairs of those oversized denim shorts with suspenders hanging off a fence nearby. A man with a bright yellow western shirt and a dusty black hat tipped far back on his head waved absently at us, his attention focused on repairing his large, padded barrel with duct tape. The smell of it cut through the bovine funk and made my heart race, but I tried not to let it show on my face.

A kid ran up to us the second we were inside the arena. He was a barely legal beanpole with a lot of wild strawberry blond hair sticking out from under his hat and a pink Hawaiian shirt over his protective vest. His flushed face was a warzone between armies of freckles and acne under the now familiar red and white greasepaint and he had a Christmas-morning gleam in his eyes.

"Draw's up," the kid said. "I pulled Krakatoa!"

"Damn, son," Sage replied, slapping the kid's bony shoulder. "Why you gotta poach my bull like that?"

"You got Ghostface Killah," the kid replied. "And you're first out so you'd better hurry."

"Right," Sage said. "Gimme a minute."

"I'm ok," I said, watching the kid run towards a set of metal stairs leading up to a platform above the livestock pens that looked out over the arena. "I can take care of myself."

"It's no problem," Sage said, taking my arm again. "Lemme just get you situated."

We passed through a narrow gate and into a boxed-off section of seating on the left side of that platform. There was only one empty chair, and Sage gestured for me to take it.

"Enjoy the show," he said. "Wash'll come and get you after, ok?"

"Will he be ok?" I asked. "His knee doesn't seem so good."

"Course he will," Sage said. "Don't you worry, your man's gonna be just fine."

But I saw a quick flash of fleeting doubt in Sage's eyes that told me he was worried too.

Then he turned away and was gone, and I was left alone with a group of curious strangers who all clearly wanted to ask about the Situation but were too polite to do so. I found myself suddenly overwhelmed by another hot rush of volcanic anger.

I was angry at myself, angry at the Situation, angry at everything. I didn't like who I had become, this weak, sniveling problem for other people to solve and I wanted to make somebody, anybody, pay. I could feel my nails cutting into my sweating palms as I clenched my fists to stop myself from asking the little old lady next to me what the fuck she was looking at. Then, as quickly as it came, the anger burned away leaving me feeling hollow, empty and alone.

I felt as if I'd lost my ability to imagine a real future, or next week, or even tomorrow, and I was just floundering and drowning in my own teary tarpit of hormonal dysfunction. I was surrounded by people, but I was so achingly lonely that it made me feel like I had some shameful, disfiguring disease. I found myself longing for the false security of a mid-range franchise hotel room with minibar snacks and cable TV and a puffy down comforter to hide under.

I had to remind myself that I was on a mission, headed somewhere safe. That there really was a plan, a person, a place where I could start a new life. Start over. Deal with the Situation, however that may play out. Put this messy, embarrassing version of myself in the rearview.

I just needed to get through this stranger-in-a-strange-land portion of our show.

My stomach did a slow roll, and I had to focus on not throwing up again.

22.

I really had no idea what to expect when Sage came strutting out into the arena, slapping outstretched hands and playing to the crowd.

"Ladies and gentlemen," a disembodied voice intoned. "Your five-time freestyle champion bullfighter, give it up for Sage Prescott!"

Sage stood out in the center of the arena, facing a large gate. He slapped his hands together, then raised them, making a beckoning "bring it on" gesture. The gate opened.

The bull that came tearing out through the open gate was much smaller than I was expecting after seeing the massive, humpbacked monsters being ridden back in Arizona. It was lean and compact and gave off a totally unexpected cloud of actual glitter when it first ran out. Its body was black, but it had a spotted white head and its horns had their sharp tips snipped off. It had shit smeared across its back end and it went straight for Sage like a train down a track. Inevitable.

Before it could hit him, Sage leapt straight up, flying like superman over the charging animal's back. He tucked into a roll as he hit the dirt and bounced right back to his limber feet. The crowd went nuts cheering as he waltzed and spun and sidestepped the furious bull. At one point he called the guy with the barrel over and stood up on it, waving to lure the bull into attacking. I had no idea how the guy inside that barrel must have been feeling being rolled across the arena like a cartoon character, but Sage just leapfrogged up and over the bull's bulky head and shoulders.

He did a few more of those near-miss dodges and then for no reason I could comprehend, it was suddenly over.

"How about eighty-nine point five points for champion Sage Prescott? EIGHTY-NINE POINT FIVE!!!"

Chase was up next, fighting a solid black bull with only one horn called Rock Steady. Instead of facing the gate where the bull was waiting, he faced away and held up his cell phone, making the "bring it" gesture over one shoulder with the other hand. I couldn't imagine that would have been a good time to take a selfie, but I guess I was wrong.

"It's the Chase Riddle signature selfie fake, ladies and gentlemen!" the announcer said as the bull came barreling out of the gate towards Chase's brightly colored back.

I never would have associated a piece of ubiquitous modern technology like a cell phone with something so seemingly old fashioned as rodeo, but I had to admit, it was a pretty good trick. He certainly had me on the edge of my seat as he just stood there grinning like a clueless tourist who wasn't about to get mowed down by 1,500 pounds of pissed-off beef.

Then, at the last possible second, he curved his body and slipped to one side, almost like he was falling but somehow, he never lost control. While Sage's body language had been tight and tense and aggressively athletic, Chase was loose and smooth like a trick skater, like Jackie Chan in *Drunken Master*. Like Buster Keaton, selling it all to the audience with a gee-whiz grin like he just couldn't believe what was happening to him. It was hard not to be impressed, but somehow, he scored lower than Sage, only 87.9. Whatever criteria the judges were using to arrive at those particular numbers was beyond me.

Two things occurred to me while I was watching this spectacle. One was that, while I'd always heard about how brutal and awful rodeo was on its non-human participants, in reality it seemed crueler in some ways and not as cruel in others. Which, to be honest, probably said more about my lack of understanding about how rural people live and interact with animals than it did about the sport itself. My personal city girl experiences with non-humans were limited to occasional encounters with other people's pets and the meat cooler in the supermarket.

The second thing that occurred to me was how cruel rodeo could be towards the humans involved. In a weird way, it was a lot like the fight game. Like porn too, if you thought about it. Seems like most people got the wrong end of the stick about why it's bad and why it isn't, but no matter how you look at it, those jobs are all about people putting their bodies through spectacular and dangerous tricks for the entertainment of others.

I had no idea how cruel it was about to get.

23.

The strawberry blond kid was in trouble.

He'd been trying for some kind of trick against the fence, but his russet red bull wasn't having it. I watched his lanky body cartwheeling through the air, baggies torn and flapping, and before my brain could register what was happening, Sage and Wash were in the arena waving their arms and belting out a rapid-fire call of *heyheyhey*.

I could tell something was wrong right away. Sage had drawn the bull off to the right and was trying to get it to run through a large open gate at one end of the arena, but Wash was doing a funny little hop step on his hurt leg as he moved in to help the younger bullfighter. That's when the bull suddenly whipped around and pinned its dark, baleful gaze on Wash.

The kid jumped up onto the fence, clinging to the top rail like a treed cat. I was trying to figure out why he had a dirty red bandana hanging out of his mouth when I realized it was a rag of skin that had been torn away from his face, exposing his bloody molars. When my eye found Wash again, I saw him try to step one way and move the other, faking the bull into charging past him. But that leg failed him, buckling under his weight. As he doubled over in pain, the bull's blocky head was rearing up and to the left, streamers of thick, milky drool trailing from its snout. Their skulls collided with a resounding crunch that rocked Wash's body backward and sent his hat flying into the stands. It was like a head-on collision between a Mack truck and a smart car and I don't have to tell you which skull was the loser in that crack up. Wash hit the dirt like he'd been shot and just laid there as the bull hooked him and ran him over.

It seemed like every bullfighter in the joint was in that arena then, along with a stoic man on horseback spinning a looped rope over his head like some kind of movie cowboy. The bull paused to take stock of the situation and seemed almost pleased with itself before casually trotting off through the gate.

Once the bull was safely contained, paramedics came rushing in with a strappy, neon yellow stretcher. Wash still hadn't moved except for a few rhythmic, full-body clenching motions like he was trying to get in a quick ab workout. An anxious hush fell over the crowd while the paramedics tended to him. The honey-voiced announcer filled the dead air with gentle platitudes.

"Doc Cutter and the Buckwell Sports Medicine Team have come to the aid of Guilford Washburn. A man who has dedicated his life to saving our riders now finds himself in need of saving. He's in God's hands now, ladies and gentlemen."

Enthusiastic applause broke out, people hooting and calling his name as Wash was lifted on the stretcher and carried out of the arena with Sage at his side. A woman I didn't know, a busty blonde with a bedazzled t-shirt that read COWBOY MOM, suddenly appeared beside me and pulled me into a hot, thickly perfumed hug. It was hard not to flinch away from this unsolicited mothering.

"He's gonna be just fine, honey," she told me. "Don't you worry."

"That boy's a tough sumbuck," offered a tiny old man whose massive belt buckle looked like it weighed more than he did. "But if you ask me, them bulls oughta be flanked. I respect Cotty, of course, but I done told him..."

"Oh, be quiet, Daddy," the woman said. "She don't need to hear none of that at a time like this."

I wanted to squirm away from her, take off running and

never look back. I wanted to grab her by her soft round shoulders and shake her and scream into her earnest, gentle face: *Don't you get it? I'M NOT WHAT YOU THINK I AM!*

I'm dangerous. A jinx. The worst thing that ever happened to everyone who ever met me. In my not-entirely-intentional transition from killer whore to deceitful madonna, I'd become someone I didn't like. I had no idea who I really was anymore.

I didn't scream at the nice lady. I just let her hold on to me while I scanned the restless crowd behind her for cops or anyone who might be a "Friend of Corbin." Anyone who looked Eastern European. Anyone who didn't seem to fit in.

And I thought, *Now what the fuck am I supposed to do?*

24.

It had been a long night. The hospital room was hushed, except for the shuffle of dusty boots around the bed and the beeps and hums of various machines. There was a strange, heavy, used-band-aid smell hovering around Wash. Like ointment and old blood and hot plastic. I held his hand, because that's what I felt like I was supposed to do. It felt weird, puffy with fluid and feverish.

Wash's eyes weren't exactly open, but they definitely weren't completely closed either. I think that was the worst part. The sputtering tube sticking out of a raw hole in his neck was forcing air in and out of his bruised chest, and the heart monitor's metronomic backbeat kept on keeping on, but his eyes were already dead.

Another one down. Another dead man. I was starting to rack up a serious body count, but yet here I was. Still slipping between the bullets, somehow. Always walking away from the burning building, like a goddamn action movie star. But what happened to that star after the movie was over? How many times can a person burn their life down before it starts to catch up with them?

Sage hadn't left my side the whole time. He was still in his dirty bullfighter jersey and shorts, hat held solemnly against his chest. His hair beneath was a warm, golden blond, short and thick as animal fur, coming to a widow's peak on his low forehead. His expression was stoic and solemn but seemed a little too studied, copied from tough-guy heroes in the movies. When a nurse came in to suck gunk out of the tube in Wash's throat, she gently herded us all out of the room and Sage took my arm just like Wyman did back at that first rodeo back in Arizona on the last day of my previous life. I found myself leaning into him, sobbing helplessly again against his broad, stiffly armored chest. He smelled like hay and sweat and high-school sports equipment.

He put his arms around me and held me gently against his upper body while subtly turning his hips away from the curve of my belly like whatever he was packing under those shorts was none of my business. It seemed deeply abnormal and confusing to be platonically embraced by yet another man who didn't seem to want to fuck me. I had so little experience interacting with men in a non-sexual manner that I felt lost, completely disconnected from my increasingly unfamiliar body.

I'm sure everyone watching thought I was crying over Wash, and I didn't do anything to contradict that impression. Because I kind of was, but also kind of wasn't.

After I'd pulled myself back together and away from Sage's asexual embrace, I looked around the crowded hallway. I was shocked by how many people were being allowed to congregate outside Wash's room, since I had always been under the impression that only one or maybe two relatives could visit an ICU patient at any given time. They were all rodeo people, faces that I recognized from the arena. Chase was there too, looking preoccupied and fiddling anxiously with a pack of cigarettes. He'd had time to change into jeans and a t-shirt, but not enough to scrub the smeared and sweaty makeup completely off his face.

Sage led me in the opposite direction towards a pair of folding chairs. The Cowboy Mom and her dad who had been sitting there quickly, silently got up to let me have a seat. A young kid who couldn't have been more than sixteen came over with a pair of battered work boots and gave them to Sage.

"And here's Wash's things," the kid said, handing over a cell phone, some keys and a folding knife.

"Thanks," Sage said, pocketing the items and sitting down beside me to unlace the dirty cleats I hadn't even noticed he was still wearing. You weren't supposed to wear shoes like that indoors, were you? It didn't seem like anybody was sticking to any kind of rules.

The kid trotted away to join a group of young men by the elevator, and Sage leaned into me as he slipped his feet into the boots.

"Listen, Angie," he said with an earnest but not entirely natural tone that made me think he'd been practicing whatever he was about to say next. "I'm gonna take care of you. You ain't gotta worry about nothing. I'm gonna get you and your baby to Harlan no matter what happens. That's a promise."

"How did you know...?" I trailed off, suddenly feeling cold and paranoid.

If he knew where I was going, who else did? Surely some of these cowboy types had to be cozy enough with law enforcement to at least know about the Corbin thing. I could see several older men looking down at their phones and felt sure that they were watching videos of Corbin swearing to hunt me down, or reading some kind of interstate BOLO with my picture or stills from that incriminating security camera footage. Or maybe that cop's body at the rest stop had finally been tied to me somehow.

"Wash wasn't making a lot of sense in the ambulance," Sage said. "But the one thing he kept repeating to me was that you needed to get to Harlan. Something about an abusive ex...?"

He let that questioning tone trail off like he was waiting for me to fill him in. I had no idea what Wash may or may not have told him, but I had to think fast, to come up with a simple, consistent story that would play off his sympathies while also making an airtight case for why it had to be kept a secret, especially from cops.

"That's right," I said. I was still kind of crying for more reasons than I could name and didn't make any effort to stop. "When he found out about the baby, he wanted me to…"

I trailed off, cupping my belly and looking away. The Situation kicked me the way somebody would kick you under the table to silently tell you to shut the fuck up. I could see Chase watching me from the other side of the hallway as he took a quick swig from a slim pocket flask.

"He wanted you to have an abortion because he knew the baby wasn't his," Sage whispered with an expression that was halfway between wonder and horror, taking the narrative football and running with it. "Course a man like Wash couldn't allow something like that, so he had to protect the two of you at all costs. No wonder he's been so secretive about the woman in his life these past few months."

I had to admit, that was a good angle, one I hadn't thought of. It was amazing how I'd never once said that Wash was responsible for the Situation, but it was starting to feel true. Even to me.

"Thing is," I said, leaning into Sage. This was where the whole story could go off the rails "My ex, he's a cop."

"Is that right?" Sage asked, his expression unreadable.

"He used his connections to spy on me and try to control me," I said. "That's why I could never go to the cops about everything he's done to me."

I was watching his face and body language for cues like I was trying to help a nervous performer keep his wood. Trying to judge what was making him harder and what was cooling him off. He hadn't lost his erection completely, but it was fading.

I had to come up with something fast.

"He has all the judges in..." I almost said L.A. but stopped myself, thinking of Wash's reaction to the mention of my hometown. "...Chicago in his pocket. You can't believe how corrupt it is there. If he finds me, he'll have my baby taken away and there won't be anything I can do to stop him."

"Wash ain't got no close blood relations outside of Harlan and Winnie," Sage told me. "But he was like family to me and that means you are too, of course. Both of you."

He put his hand on my belly.

"I ain't gonna tell nobody," he said. "Well, almost nobody."

"What do you mean by that?" I frowned.

He tipped his chin towards Chase, who was now staring out the window while capping the flask.

"Thing is," he said. "Chase is the only one besides Wash who knows how to get to Harlan's place."

"Can't you get directions on your phone?"

He smirked.

"Nope," he said. "Ain't no address. You look on a map of that area, you won't see nothing but wild land. Which is the whole point of going there in the first place, right?"

He was right, of course. I'd heard the phrase "off the grid" so many times, but the meaning of it was just starting to really sink in. Was I sure this was a good idea? Was anything?

"I'm sorry..." I stammered. "I... I need some air."

I couldn't get out of there fast enough.

25.

Standing in the narrow lobby by the gift shop, I stared at a sad cluster of cheap teddy bears and thought about leaving for what had to be the hundredth time. Just walking the fuck away. The leaving, the act itself, seemed like the right thing to do in the face of this wild cancerous lie that couldn't possibly end well for anyone involved. But then what?

I didn't have an answer to that question. But in the end, I didn't need one, because four bad men walked in the door and herded me right back into the questionable embrace of my mistaken identity.

You could tell right away who was the boss. Sixties maybe, tall, clean-shaven and sunburned with wide, scarecrow shoulders. Same ubiquitous straw hat as pretty much everybody else but me and this big gold buckle that said TOP BULL. He had long, yellow teeth like a horse and his too-blue eyes burned like pilot lights behind aviator style glasses. He moved like an old fighter, like every bone hurt but he was too tough to show it.

By his side was a younger, hatless man who had the same scarecrow build and horsey teeth as the Top Bull guy but with dark eyes and no glasses. He seemed tightly wound and anxious, while the older man was stoic and disconcertingly calm in a way that reminded me of Niko, the killer who shot Vukasin.

The other two were straight up muscle. Good-ole-boys, similar as brothers. Tall like their boss, but all yoked up and surly like they were annoyed to be here instead of at the gym. Could have been working for Vukasin if they'd been dressed in cheap, shiny suits instead of jeans and button downs. They could not have cared less about me.

Chase came strolling past me, unlit cigarette between his narrow lips. When he saw the four men, he stopped like he'd walked into an invisible wall.

Some kind of hushed, intense conversation ensued between Chase and the Top Bull guy then while the henchmen moved casually around to flank him and cut off any escape.

The muscle seemed to be working together on casually maneuvering him towards the door and he clearly didn't want to go with them. He slipped to one side and then the other, shrugging off their big square hands and putting his own palms up and out in a placating gesture. Never overtly fighting them, but never letting them get a hold of him.

There was a security guard sitting at a desk on the opposite side of the lobby who didn't seem even remotely interested in what was going on with them, his attention riveted on a television screen showing a conservative commentator explaining how the world was going to hell in a handbasket.

Chase had turned towards the television screen as he continued to try and talk his way out of whatever was happening, when the commentator told his rapt audience that they weren't going to believe this and I don't have to tell you what was the next thing that popped up on the screen, do I?

Of fucking course, it was the footage of me shooting the cop.

The video was grainy and I would have been impossible to recognize even if I hadn't worked so hard to change my look, but the sight of it goosed me unconsciously forward anyway.

26.

I didn't exactly want to get in the middle of whatever was going on here, but I also knew that as much as Sage wanted to make himself out to be my new hero, Chase was the one I really needed.

The thought of having my last chance of finding Harlan snatched away right in front of me unleashed another involuntary flood of volcanic hormonal fury. A forgotten ball point pen lay on the scuffed tile near the security desk and I picked it up, fully intending to stab somebody in the neck for trying to get in my way. I had actually taken more than one step in the direction of the men with the pen clutched in a white-knuckled grip, but I forced myself to slow down, to breathe, to think.

Don't be stupid, I thought. Be strategic.

I was still mad as hell, but I knew what I needed to do.

I dropped the pen and then half ran, half staggered over to where Chase was standing. I threw myself blindly against him, gently turning him away from the TV screen, which now featured a new interview with Bill Corbin.

Corbin looked like his grief was eating him alive. The fanatical glint in his eyes seemed to unnerve even the interviewer, who was clearly on his side about me getting what I deserved. But I didn't have time to think about that now.

"Chase," I said, clutching his arm and working up to some thick, hiccupping sobs that were only half fake. "Oh God isn't it awful? Do you think Wash is gonna be ok? I'm so worried about him..."

"Course you are, darlin'," he replied, sliding a protective

arm around me while side-eyeing the goons. Never once did he look up at the screen. "We all are. Anyway we better git, in case he wakes up and needs his loving woman and precious little baby by his side."

The Top Bull guy was clearly annoyed by my interference, but getting rough with a distraught pregnant lady in a busy public hospital was a bad idea by anybody's standards. The security guy was finally paying attention to us now that the TV show had cut to commercial.

Chase deftly maneuvered me around like we were dancing, sweeping me into the open elevator and never taking his eyes off the bad men.

"What the hell was that all about," I asked once the elevator doors closed.

"You don't want to know," he replied, sliding the never lit cigarette back in the pack with shaking hands.

"Try me," I said. "I can handle it."

He looked over at me with a skeptical squint.

"Let's just say I took something that wasn't mine," he said. "Only it didn't work out like I had planned."

"What," I said. "Did you rob a bank?"

He shook his head.

"Nothing that glamorous," he replied.

The door opened on the ICU floor, and it seemed like the crowd in the hall had mostly flowed back into Wash's room. Chase gestured for me to get out first, then sidled over to the window overlooking the parking lot. When I joined him, I could see the Top Bull guy and the younger man having some kind of argument while the muscle twins stood there blank and unplugged, thinking about protein powder or buckle bunnies or whatever.

"Who are those guys?" I asked.

"That there is Big Dale Fleischhauer," he said, like that was supposed to mean something to me. When he saw my baffled expression, he elaborated unhelpfully. "Stock contractor."

"Right," I said.

"That's the guy who provides the animals for rodeos," he said. "In his case, bucking bulls."

"And I guess that must be Little Dale with him."

"Nope," he said. "That's Ty. He's the runt of the litter and clearly feeling like he needs to nut up and move up a rung, now that Little Dale's gone home to Jesus."

I watched Big Dale poke a finger into the center of Ty's chest and then turn away. One of the lunkheads opened the back door of a waiting car for him while the other got into the driver's seat. Big Dale gripped the crown of his hat and ducked into the back seat, folding his long stiff legs slowly into the vehicle. The one lunkhead closed the back door and joined the other in the front while Ty hovered dejectedly, seemingly hoping for some kind of reprieve or change of heart.

"But what does any of this have to do with you?" I asked as the car peeled out of the lot.

Ty, having been given a clear message of some sort, started walking away, his whole body clenched like a fist.

"Well, you see, Angie," Chase said like he was gearing up to tell an exciting story to a group of kindergarteners. "It's the manner of Little Dale's departure from this earthly domain that's at issue here." His accent seemed to flex and strengthen as he spoke. "Specifically, my role in said departure."

"You killed him," I said.

"I may be a no-account drunkard and an unrepentant back-door man," he replied, trying to maintain the smooth rhythm of his story while his uneasy eyes darted back to the window and away. Both Ty and the car were already gone. "But I ain't no killer."

Of course, I couldn't fault him if he actually was, but I wasn't about to tell him why. I just let him continue.

“It went down like this. Little Dale and me, well, we were supposed to liberate some genetics off of a competitor who outbid his daddy. Big Dale don’t like to lose.”

“Genetics?”

“Semen,” he replied with a wink and a sharp smirk that lifted one stiffly waxed curl of his mustache, in full showman mode now. “It was a pick-and-mix lot from several top athletes, but the crown jewel was thirteen straws of Bad Day at Black Rock. Ol’ Bad Day’s been dead for a decade now, but he was a legend in his time. One of the all-time rankest, only been covered once. He sired a handful of Big Dale’s top money champions, including Midnight Rider and Black Dynamite. Those thirteen straws of frozen gold were the last ones left on God’s green earth and Big Dale wasn’t about to let anyone else have ’em. That’s where yours truly comes in.

“Truth be told,” he said, making me think what he was about to say next was anything but. “Little Dale was always kind of a fuck up, but he was pretty just like his mama and could do no wrong in Daddy’s eyes. Anyway, that’s how come I got sent along with him to make sure everything went smooth. Course, it didn’t. Guns was drawn and well, Little Dale wound up on the wrong end. He just wasn’t used to sidestepping trouble like I am.”

Over the course of spinning this yarn, I could see Chase loosening up, tension leaving his neck and shoulders. He was clearly a natural-born storyteller, and everybody defaults to what they’re good at when things get stressful. I tended to fall back on my world-famous blowjobs, he clearly loved a Tall Tale. I wondered how much of what he was telling me was true and how much was him constructing his own narrative in which he was the wily trickster hero who always managed to give trouble the slip while flashing a sly wink at the audience.

"Honestly, I think Big Dale was more sore about the fact that I wasn't able to save them straws." He smiled and shook his head. "But I tell you what, darlin'. I showed you mine, now you gotta show me yours."

"What do you mean?"

"I mean, what's your angle here?" he asked. "We all know Wash is a sucker for headstrong redheads and he's been real tight-lipped about his love life lately, so one can't help but put two and two together." He leaned close to me and dropped his voice to a whisper, even though there were just the two of us in the hall. "Only it don't really add up right in my book. Call it a gut feeling, but I think there's more to this than you're letting on."

"What makes you say that?" I asked, trying to keep my shit together.

"Well for starters, the look on your face right now." He grinned. "Do yourself a favor and don't take up poker."

"It's…" I looked away. Anywhere but at him. "…complicated."

"Oh, I don't doubt that," he replied. "And don't worry, Angie. Whatever you got going on is between you and Wash. Don't got nothing to do with me."

"Listen, Chase," I said, placing a nervous hand on my belly. "I need to get to Harlan. If you've been paying attention to all the gossip flying around, I guess I don't have to explain why."

"Guess not," he said.

"Anyway, Sage tells me you're the only one besides Wash who knows the way. Is that true?"

"Yeah," he said, nodding like the truth of that statement was just sinking in. "Yeah, that's right."

"Will you help me?"

For a minute, I thought maybe he'd say no. Not that I'd blame him, of course. That was the only sensible answer. He certainly wasn't trying to sell himself as anybody's hero the way

Sage was and, based on the story about the bull semen, he definitely had a pretty strong sense of self-preservation.

"Well, seeing as how you just saved my bacon from Big Dale's frying pan," Chase said. "I suppose I owe you one, don't I?"

We could hear passionate, singsong voices coming from the far end of the hallway where Wash's room was. He practically had an entire church choir in there. It sounded like they were praying.

I slowed up a bit, feeling awkward about another potentially confusing religious interaction that would mark me as Other in the eyes of people who I really needed on my side. Of course, the disconcertingly sharp Chase picked up on my discomfort right away. I was really going to have to watch myself around him.

"I don't go in for that kinda thing either," he said. "I figure if there is a god, all the praying in the world ain't gonna change his mind about me."

I didn't say *me too*, but I didn't need to.

The two of us lingered for a minute in the doorway while they finished up their long, meandering and seemingly ad-libbed prayer. I found myself thinking of the phrase "fruit of thy womb" from the only prayer I knew and how strange that really was. Like my belly was a bowl full of pretty peaches and apples and grapes, like some old still life painting in a museum, rather than the bloody caldron of terrifying creation that it actually was. Better not to think about it, just like it was better not to think about "the hour of our death."

I was getting to be a real expert in not thinking about things.

Everybody said amen then, and we walked into Wash's room together.

27.

Sage was standing over the hospital bed, weirdly happy and puppy-excited for someone watching over a comatose friend. He took Wash's hand.

"You've been my biggest hype man this year," he said. "Driving me to be better and push harder and follow my dream. Well, listen to this!"

He held up his phone and thumbed a button on the screen.

"Sage Prescott?" A woman's voice, warm and gently accented. "This here is Taryn Coil from the PRCA. I'm calling to congratulate you on making it into the top ten for…um…bullfighter for NFR…"

He pushed another button on the phone, cutting off the voice.

"How do you like that?" he asked. "Course, I ain't been picked for sure, not yet anyway, but the next round of voting is next week and I swear to you, Wash, I'm gonna make it through. You'll see. I'm gonna go pick up your new vest from Buck and wear it in your honor in the NFR."

Silence. Sage squeezed Wash's limp fingers.

"You may be watching me on TV this year," he said. "But you're gonna bounce back stronger than ever and next year, we'll all be watching you!"

For a moment, it seemed like Wash was responding to this news. His strange, flat eyes rolled from side to side and the steady backbeat of his heart monitor kicked it up a notch.

"He can hear you!" the Cowboy Mom said in a reverent whisper. "Praise God!"

"You do hear me, don't you?" Sage said, squeezing harder as he leaned in. "I ain't gonna let nothing happen to Angie and the baby. Swear to God, I won't."

"Listen up," the nurse was saying, gentle hand on Sage's big shoulder. "I'm gonna need all y'all to step out for just a moment, ok?"

"Sure," he said, looking anything but sure. "Yes, ok, you bet."

Doctors started rushing into the room that we had just vacated. When the heart monitor's frantic, death metal beat resolved into a single droning tone that only meant one thing, I felt like I was the one who was dead.

I let Sage put his long, sinewy arms around me again as the nurse told us how sorry she was and that Wash was with God in heaven now. I pressed my face into Sage's damp armpit, mostly to hide the fact that I wasn't crying. Whatever tear regulatory system I had left had clearly broken long ago, running like a leaky faucet at random, inconvenient times, and then other times dry as dust with no logic or meaning behind it. I just felt cold and hopeless, like a lump of meat against him. He was crying in his own way, just a single tough-guy tear and a determined grimace, and I couldn't help but think that was intentional on his part. Look sad, but not too sad. Man sad, not messy, hysterical, pregnant lady sad.

It seemed like everyone wanted to hug me, touch me, pray for me and assure me that if I needed anything at all, they would be there for me, but it all felt like it was happening to someone else. Which, in a way, it was. None of them knew who I really was.

I needed to get the hell out of there, but I didn't have to say anything. Sage and Chase wordlessly flanked me and eased me towards the elevator just like the two thugs had been trying to do to Chase. I let them, unable to think of anything else.

28.

When we came up to Chase's truck in the far back of the lot, I almost laughed out loud. It was not exactly a low-profile getaway ride.

It was covered with a gaudy, colorful wrap featuring a selfie of Chase giving a thumbs up to the camera with a furious, charging bull in the background. Garish, bright purple and yellow western-style letters read CHASE RIDDLE, PROFESSIONAL BULLFIGHTER and FIGHT RANK, MAKE BANK! It had Texas plates and tons of bumper stickers from rodeos all over the country.

All four tires were slashed.

"Fuck," Chase said.

He and Sage were arguing over what to do next, making a clever plan or something I suppose, but I just stood there feeling more inert and useless than ever. There was a grackle high-stepping along the hot asphalt and occasionally checking me out with a tilted head and one pale eye. I felt inexplicably judged and wanted to explain that none of this was my fault, except it all was. Sage was texting on his phone, thumbs flying, and eventually, some kind of decision was made.

When Sage ran off to jump into the passenger seat of somebody else's truck, Chase got on his own phone, making arrangements to deal with his tires. I didn't have a phone. I just watched the grackle and cried silently without feeling anything.

Chase didn't want to wait by his truck, and he didn't say it was because he was nervous about Ty or the Top Bull guy coming back to slash him to match his tires, but he didn't have to. He walked me over to a small bench, told me to sit tight and then took off and left me alone without explanation.

Sitting there on the bench, in a town I'd never heard of in a state I'd never visited and feeling like a broken Rubik's cube that nobody could solve, I knew I needed to take some kind of action to break out of this toxic passivity.

I like to believe that I would have too, only a cop car pulled up to the front of the hospital.

Of course, they weren't there for me. Why would they be?

Or were they?

Maybe the security guard who had been watching that interview with Corbin had recognized me? I ducked and turned my head to hide behind my hair, pushing the Jackie O sunglasses up my nose. I got to my feet as quickly as I could, desperately needing to move, to run, to just get the hell out of there and not worry about where I was going.

I almost ran right into Chase.

"I got you some fries," he said, holding up a grease-stained paper bag. "When my ex was pregnant, she always craved salt." He paused, looking first at me, then over at the two cops getting out of their car, then back again. "You ok?"

He couldn't see my eyes, but he obviously didn't need to. Just like he'd somehow psychically picked up on me wanting fries, he was also reading my reaction to the cops like it was a neon sign.

"Don't worry, Angie," he said. "Them boys are here to transfer that sorry ass chucklefuck who got shot by somebody's grandma while trying to rob the Walmart. They ain't here for you."

"Of course not," I replied, unable to stop watching them out of the corner of my eye as they went inside. "Why would they be?"

"Why indeed?" he asked, handing me the bag.

That's when Sage showed up driving Wash's truck.

"Get in," he said.

29.

"What the hell were you thinking?" Chase asked, passing me his phone over his shoulder and glaring at Sage over the tops of his rainbow mirror shades. "Why don't you just call up Angie's ex and invite him over for Sunday fucking dinner?"

I was sitting in the back seat of the truck, watching the endless road unfurl between their hatless heads. Sage was behind the wheel, long dirty neck hunched down and his bristly golden hair still brushing the roof of the cab. Chase rode shotgun, wild dark curls starting to thin a little at the crown and in desperate need of a barber. I looked down at the phone Chase had handed to me.

On the cracked screen was an Instagram post by Sage featuring a photo of me leaning against Chase's gaudy truck. That is to say, it was a photo of the Situation. Also, my tits with Wash's mama's cross between them. You couldn't see my face, just licks of coppery hair, and he'd added some kind of pretty filter that made my perpetually flushed, hormonal skin look pale and flawless. He must have snapped that photo in front of the hospital without my noticing. The caption below read:

> *Wash I know you're looking down from heaven and I just want you to know that I'm protecting your little family with everything I got, keeping them safe from that cowardly woman-beater who tried to force her to abort your baby! We're on our way to Hookin' B right now to pick up your vest, which, God willing, I plan to wear in your honor in the NFR. #GodBlessBabyWashburn*

"I didn't show her face," Sage said, shrugging. "Or use her name."

"You know I love you like a brother," Chase replied. "But sometimes I swear you ain't got enough sense to make a fucking nickel. I mean, look, I get it. I realize that you need to be out there selling your ass like a two-dollar whore for them NFR votes, but..." He was clearly trying to rein in his temper, chewing at that preposterous waxed mustache. "Would you maybe for one fucking second consider a single human being other than yourself? Like maybe don't tell the whole goddamn internet exactly where we're going?"

I knew this wasn't all chivalry on my behalf. Chase had reasons not to want anyone to know where he was going either. Particularly not Big Dale.

"I ain't doing this for votes," Sage said, voice tight and defensive, keeping his expression neutral and his eyes on the road as he drove. "I'm helping Angie because it's the right thing to do. Not that you'd know anything about that."

"Beware of practicing your piety before others in order to be seen by them," Chase intoned in a theatrical, preacher's cadence. "For then you have no reward from your Father in heaven."

Sage laughed and rolled his eyes, breaking the tension between them.

"You did *not* just throw scripture at me, you godless heathen!"

"God may not love me," Chase replied. "But the ladies dang sure do."

"Hey," I said from the back seat, irritated and frustrated and hating how useless I felt. "Am I even a person back here?"

"Sorry, Angie," Sage said. "Don't mind Chase, he's never been around a decent woman before."

I wanted to tell him that he wasn't around one then either, but made myself take a few deep breaths and asked if we could make another pit stop instead.

*

When we pulled over at a rest area that was clearly designed by the same baffling genius who put up the decorative metal amoebas that took out Wash's knee, I felt a cold, ugly panic scrabbling inside my chest like it was looking for a way out. I crushed it down hard, gritting my teeth and hauling myself out of the back seat to make my way towards the bathroom.

When I got back, Sage was not there but Chase was leaning against the truck like I had been in the Instagram photo, drinking out of a brown paper bag and looking at his cell phone. When he looked up, he toasted me with the bag.

"I'd offer you a snort, but…" He gestured at the Situation. "You know."

"Right," I said, looking up at the endless sky. I didn't bother to tell him I'd never been much of a drinker even before the whole uterine occupation thing. "It's fine."

"You're quite a hit on the ol' Insta," he said. "Hashtag God Bless Baby Washburn!"

"Oh god," I said, trying to figure how easy it would be to Sherlock Holmes whatever scraps of digital clues were contained in that viral photo together into something that would lead Bill Corbin right to me. "So much for keeping a low profile."

"Sage ain't a natural born asshole like I am," he said. "He's just all about the Sage Prescott Show."

"I bet you're not really the asshole you want everyone to believe you are," I replied. "Any more than Sage is the Instagram hero he wants everyone to think he is."

"Guess that remains to be seen," he said, taking another swig. "Don't it?"

30.

Were we in Wyoming? Utah? When you look up those states you see gorgeous, postcard images of the rugged American west, all sunset-lit and majestic. Buttes and shit. But driving through them was like driving on the surface of a grim and hostile planet. Endless, bleak, soul-destroying roads to nowhere under an unforgiving sky that was way too big and too blue. Scrappy tufts of thirsty vegetation and power lines and maybe that might be some mountains off in the distance or maybe just my roadsick imagination. I'd drift off in the truck's back seat and when I woke up, it would look like we hadn't moved at all. Like we were stuck in some kind of Twilight Zone time loop. Going a hundred miles an hour and getting nowhere.

Then Sage took a hard right onto a barely there dirt road. There was no street sign, just a handmade metal plaque featuring a letter B with stylized horns. At first the land on either side of the road was a patchwork of flat green pasture with stretches of dry, dead weeds and a few scrappy, twisted trees but as we drove, the ground started slanting upward towards a distant jumble of loose rocks like scattered teeth after a fistfight between giants. I could see some weathered structures on both sides of the road, barns or garages of some kind. Maybe a glimpse of a house on the far left or maybe that was just wishful thinking on my part. Maybe we were the last three humans left on Earth. Four, if you counted the Situation.

Turns out that wasn't the case, though we would have been better off if it was.

We eventually came upon a large, rough-hewn wooden arch

with a bleached cow skull nailed to the center just below that same horned B crafted from twisted black iron. I kept thinking we had to be getting close to wherever we were going soon, but I dozed off again and when I woke up from another bout of fitful, uncomfortable sleep, we still weren't there. We were on a steepening road that wound between the giant's teeth. The land on both sides of the road was loose and rocky, prone to tiny avalanches of dust and pebbles brought on by the vibration of the truck engine.

When we finally reached our destination, Sage drove through an open gate in a sturdy metal fence and eased the truck into a spot between a massive multi-horse trailer and a stack of additional fence pieces. Dead ahead was a clean, well-maintained barn with the same horned B symbol over the broad, open door. Off to our left was another gate and a neat gravel path leading to a large, surprisingly modern home. I don't know what I was expecting, something more rustic I guess, but this was a cascade of sleek, angular glass-and-steel origami that wouldn't have looked out of place in the Hollywood Hills. Clinging to the sharp lip of a vertiginous cliff, the house overlooked a glittering snake of a river that had cut deep into the layer-cake rock over eons of forgotten time. Beyond that, acres of wild land and a faint, distant hint of some kind of human civilization on the far horizon.

On the right was a short dirt road leading down to a complicated tangle of paddocks and gates and a maze of those big metal fence pieces linked together. Beyond that, a flat tongue of green pasture with a winding fence along the cliff edge to keep any animals from getting too close.

When we got out of the truck, I went over to look through the bars of the fence and a series of bulky black heads popped up out of the grass to turn my way. Cows, maybe a dozen of them visible from where I was standing. They seemed like females to my untrained eye, but they all had that murderous glint in their eyes, like they'd be just as happy to trample and kill me as their male counterparts. One of the ones standing closest to me had a largish calf beside her and seemed particularly interested in facilitating my immediate demise. Even though there were several layers of fencing between us, I was tempted to jump back into the truck and lock the doors.

I might have done it too, but a couple came down the path from the house to greet us.

The woman was maybe a few years younger than me, a statuesque redhead with a thick, windswept braid over one freckled shoulder. She didn't have that flashy, cowgirl stripper look like the buckle bunnies I'd seen back in Arizona or the #blessed Christian Instagram Girl style that seemed more popular in Oklahoma. She looked like she just stepped out of a Ralph Lauren spread in *Vogue*, the kind that made Europeans want to buy a ridiculously expensive cowboy hat. Her lean, angular body was draped in cream linen and buttery brown suede and tasteful turquoise jewelry that matched her eyes. She was beautiful in that striking, slightly off-kilter, former runway model kind of way. Neck a little too long, eyes a little too wide set, nose a little too sharp. No trace of makeup, and no nail polish on her strong, hardworking hands. She looked like a woman to be reckoned with.

I felt like I was becoming an expert on the taxonomy of blond men ever since I crash landed on Planet Rodeo, and the redhead's husband was that peculiar kind of natural blond whose hair never darkened from childish cornsilk. It just crept back off his forehead and got thinner, exposing his shiny pink scalp. He wore faded Wranglers and a starched button-up with that horned letter B and the words "HOOKIN B RANCH" above the left breast pocket, a humble and unassuming uniform indistinguishable from just about every other man I'd encountered in and around the rodeo. His pale blue eyes seemed nearly lashless, disappearing into a nest of deep crow's feet as he smiled and waved at us. He held a straw cowboy hat, twisting the brim in his raw pink fists.

"I sure am sorry to hear about Wash," he said. "I'm Buck Burr. It's an honor and blessing to be able to help you and the baby, Angie."

I found it deeply distressing that someone I'd never met already knew my name. Even if it wasn't really my real name. Or my real fake name for that matter.

Who even was I?

I stuck my sweaty hand out to him, but he ignored it and pulled me into a warm bear hug. The Situation kicked out against him like it was as uncomfortable with all this physical affection as I was.

"You got yourself a little bullfighter in there," he said, placing a wide palm on my belly. "He's making rounds already, Mikayla!"

"Ain't that precious?" The redhead came forward with a warm, crooked grin, klieg-light charisma bathing me and making me feel the way you do when a famous person talks to you. "The Lord has yet to bless us with children of our own, but Wash was family." She reached out and took Sage's hand. I couldn't help but notice Chase hanging back a little, eyes hidden behind those rainbow mirror shades. "All our boys are family. You could be too, if you wanted."

"Thanks," I said, unsure of what else to say.

"We need to get her..." Sage started to say, and then paused, sending a meaningful glance my way and lowered his voice to a dramatic whisper, like a child. "....to Harlan." He squeezed

Mikayla's hand and then let it go to sling a protective arm around my shoulders. "On account of the fact that her no-good ex is still trying to find her."

"The one who tried to force her to have an abortion?" Mikayla asked, some flicker of unknown emotion like the shadow of a moth dancing briefly against the blaze of her charm. "Well, they're both safe now, thank God!"

"Thanks to you too, Sage," Buck said. "I'm proud of you for stepping up like you have. We all are."

"Damn straight," Chase said with a sarcastic twist to his mustached lips. "Every fucking one of us."

"You watch that language, Chase Riddle," Mikayla said, making me think of Hank. "We got little ears here, don't we?"

I really didn't want to think about what the Situation may or may not have been able to hear over the past couple of months, so I changed the subject.

"Got anything to eat?" I asked. "It seems like I'm hungry all the time now."

"Course you are," Buck said. "Lemme get the grill fired up."

After a huge meal of steak, steak and steak with a little bit of salad "for vitamins," the men sat around the table drinking beer while Mikayla and I stuck with homemade iced tea from a thick glass pitcher decorated with abstract yellow shapes that suggested chunky lemon wedges. Buck bragged about his cattle in ways that made no sense to me, but I just nodded a lot and tried to act impressed. Sage bragged about the NFR nomination and how it was a sure thing, pretty much ordained by God at this point and how it's what Wash would have wanted. Chase the storyteller didn't brag about anything, instead keeping his mouth uncharacteristically shut as he racked up a collection of empty beer cans beside his plate.

Mikayla just quietly, gracefully took care of everyone, clearing plates and providing refills and occasionally letting Buck pull her into his lap and kiss her long, freckled neck, calling her babygirl.

"Ain't she just the best?" he asked me, like she was another one of his exceptionally well-bred cows.

"Go on now, Daddy," she said, extricating herself from his grasp. "Why don't you take Sage down to the shop?"

"C'mon, Angie," Sage said. "You're gonna want to see this."

Between the barn and the fenced-in pasture was a small, rectangular metal building Buck referred to as the shop. Inside it was cluttered and chaotic, filled with an eclectic mix of tools and equipment. There was an airbrush rig and a wild rainbow of disorganized paint bottles. There were whole cow hides with the hair still on and rolls of Velcro and stacks of white plastic shells like giant Pringles potato chips. There was a huge pegboard filled with various dangerous-looking implements for leatherworking and other mysterious purposes. A weird metal contraption with a single wheel, wide handles and a pair of horns was precariously balanced on top of an upside-down feed trough, various ornately tooled belts and reins and hatbands draped all over it. The space was lit by three seemingly random bulbs hanging from the corrugated ceiling and although there were no windows, a big fan set into a grate high up on the back wall let slanting bars of setting sunlight in between its unmoving blades.

All along the opposite wall were rows of those stiff, protective bullfighter vests hanging from hooks. All sizes, all colors. Some had just the plain white plastic plates on the back with the Hookin B logo in the lower left corner and some were customized with words or symbols or various ornate designs.

"Here it is," Buck said, taking down one of the vests and holding it out to Sage.

The back of the vest had been airbrushed with metallic blues, purples, and silver in a swirling spiral vortex. It had WASHBURN spelled out across the top and the words SPIN CYCLE twisting inward towards the center point of the vortex. The front of the vest was two-thirds black and a third airbrushed with the same metallic blue paint. There was a silver cross in the center and below that in neat white cursive script "No greater love has any man than this, that he lay down his life for his friends –John 15:13."

Sage took the vest and for a moment, the three of us just stood there saying nothing. The vest retained the shape of a human chest even when it wasn't being worn, which made its obvious hollow emptiness feel like an accusation.

Yet another person who was no longer around because of me.

Of course, there was no way to know if what happened to Wash would have happened if he never met me. Maybe that bum knee was gonna give no matter what and the fact that he banged it up defending my deeply questionable honor had nothing to do with his death. It's not like he didn't know he was in a dangerous sport, in fact that was kind of the whole point. So why did I still feel like fucking poison?

"Hard to believe he's gone," Sage said softly, sliding his hand inside the empty vest where Wash's heart should have been.

"God bless you for everything you're doing to honor his memory," Buck replied. "Let's see about getting you fitted."

I looked away while Sage and Buck fussed with straps and side panels, adjusting and fitting the vest to Sage's long, lanky body.

"You got about six inches on him," Buck was saying, tightening the straps. "But it's all leg. Your torsos are almost exactly the same length. Though I might could add a bit more height on that rib protector for you."

"I got all the protection I need," Sage replied, touching two fingers to the cross in the middle of his chest. "Hey, why don't you grab a pic?"

Buck fished a phone in a bulky, yellow protective case from his back pocket and I backed away from him like he was holding a live snake.

"Don't worry, Angie," Sage said. "You won't be in the picture."

"Fine," I replied. "I'm going to get some air."

I staggered out through the metal door, feeling dizzy and breathless, suffocating under the weight of too many huge, indescribable emotions. I wasn't sad and I wasn't angry, I just felt everything too intensely and all at once.

How did I get roped into playing a saintly pregnant widow on Sage's preposterous and ongoing Kowboy Kardashian show, and how could I write myself out of the narrative? Was any of this echoing back to the star of my own personal reality show? I needed to find out.

Mikayla let me use a laptop tucked into a little study nook at the far end of the big sunny kitchen. I made up some story about email, but of course I really wanted to see what was going on with Corbin.

The rest of L.A. may have moved on, but Corbin was not going to let it go. He had a YouTube channel devoted to angry rants about me, increasingly twisted conspiracies about why I was still at large, and tips from supporters, who apparently referred to themselves as "Friends of Corbin." There were no references to the #GodBlessBabyWashburn thing, and he hadn't made any obvious connection yet between the "friend" found dead at the truck stop and the object of his vengeful desire, but that probably wasn't going to last.

Watching him was mesmerizing. He was wounded and crazy but not wrong about me, really. I had to tear myself away from the little screen.

31.

I poured myself some more ice tea from the pitcher on the kitchen counter and wandered out onto the back deck. I found Chase sitting on a low-slung Adirondack chair, strumming an acoustic guitar with a fat joint stuck in the corner of his mouth.

"Guess I'll keep rodeoing, fighting bulls and fucking bunnies," he crooned in a surprisingly deep, maple syrup baritone. "It's easier than waiting around to die."

"Is it though?" I asked, looking out at the distant horizon and taking a sip of tea. "I mean, don't you get tired sometimes? Don't you ever want to stop all this?"

"I dunno," Chase replied, continuing to strum that soft, melancholy tune. "I came out my momma running. That's why she named me Chase. Hell, I been running so long, I don't remember what it feels like to be still."

I nodded. Boy did I know what that was like, but I didn't say anything. Didn't have to.

"That's how I came to be the no-account rodeo bum you see before you today." He switched up the chords he was playing and sang softly. "A hobo with stars in my crown."

"You got some kind of exit strategy?" I asked. "Plans for the future?"

"Plans?" He made a soft scoffing sound, blowing pungent smoke out through flared nostrils. "I don't even know what that means."

"Me neither," I said.

"I'll tell you what I do know," he said. "This beat up old chassis ain't gonna go much longer, that's the inevitable fucking truth. There's kids out there half my age and twice as hungry. Back in my daddy's day, you just got drunk and got out there in the arena to see what you were made of. Now it's a respectable sport, with guys eating right and living clean, training night and day like it's the fucking Olympics or some shit."

I nodded, said nothing.

"I came up with the selfie fake to try and stay relevant with the younger crowd," he continued. "But it ain't sustainable, you know? Every man gets to a point in his life where he needs to start thinking about the get off."

"I'm not giving you a blowjob if that's what you're asking," I said with a smirk, ice clinking in my nearly empty glass.

"Damn, woman," he said. He sucked another draw off the joint. "I'm trying to be all philosophical and serious for a second here. I'm talking about how to end your ride. Because you hang on and hang on and keep on hanging on with every ounce of fight you got in you, but then what? How do you force yourself to let go and move on?"

"Fuck if I know," I said.

32.

I was given a room on the second floor that looked like it had never been slept in. Perfectly crisp sheets. Museum-quality antique Navajo baskets. Throw pillows with bold, southwest designs. A fat, unburned candle with a gentle scent like sage and honey.

I washed my frazzled orange hair under a wide chrome rain shower head, lathering up fistfuls of thick, pricy shampoo. I avoided looking too closely in the foggy mirror as I slicked my hair into submission with a fragrant golden oil that made it look a little more like normal human locks and not the matted mane of a neglected orangutan in a roadside zoo. It was hard not to compare it to Mikayla's glossy, naturally vibrant tresses, but it's not like I had any reason to look hot at the moment. I was a little bit worried about the dark roots that were starting to make themselves known beneath the drugstore color though. Did anyone still remember the old me? Did I?

The Situation gave me a stiff roundhouse kick to the bladder like that was the definitive answer to my question. But was that a positive answer or a negative?

I put on clean underwear and slipped Wash's cross back on over my head. I had no idea if it was bringing me good luck or bad, but I felt irrationally attached to it and didn't want to leave it off for the night.

Someone, Mikayla I assume, had laid out a nightgown for me. It was fresh and crisp, the kind of white eyelet lace deal that you wore while creeping through a spooky old house holding a candelabra and looking for ghosts. This house was nearly new and nobody's idea of gothic, but I still had the feeling there were ghosts here.

When I got under the covers, it felt almost too good to be true. Which, unsurprisingly, it was.

I dreamed about a campfire, knots popping and sending up trails of sparks into the cold starry sky. I think my old friend Didi was there, or maybe it was my mom, telling me that I needed to cut my hair, only I had my regular dark hair in the dream. I didn't want to do it, but I felt like it was for the best, so I cut the thick braid, a braid just like Mikayla's and tossed it into the fire. It burned blue.

When I woke, the campfire smell was still there. Deeply resinous and sweet, with just the slightest hint of barbecue. Was Buck grilling more steak? I thought if I had to eat any more beef, I'd grow horns.

I slipped out of my room and crept slowly down the stairs.

The sun was coming up, throwing a sullen orange glow through the massive windows, though I felt like I'd hardly slept more than an hour or two. That smoky scent was getting stronger.

"I want them top Brahmans trailered out ASAP, ok?" Buck was saying into a cell phone. "And what's the calf count down the back west?" He paused, nodded. "Right, well, hell if I know. You're just gonna have to cut that fence and let God sort 'em, son. Tanner…? Tanner! Shit."

He tossed the phone on the table.

"There goes the signal," he said.

There was a sharp rapping on the door and Buck opened it to reveal a dramatically backlit man in a cowboy hat. I realized two things at once, first that man was a cop, orange light glinting off the badge on the front of his hat. Second was that the sun wasn't coming up. It was still the middle of the night, and the night was on fire.

It was beautiful and terrifying.

33.

I figured that my number was up, and wondered if the cop would let me get dressed or just cuff me in this nightgown. The apocalyptic hell-lighting seemed like an appropriate cinematic backdrop for my arrest.

Turned out he didn't care about me at all.

"Fire's jumped the road," the cop said, taking off his hat and swiping a hand through his sweaty black hair. "It's burning clear down 19 and past the Haydens'. Tires melted on the prowler coming across Kelton, so there's no getting back into Landry until the county boys show up to beat back the main line. We got mandatory evac in effect down in Ohlsville, but as of zero two hundred they're saying everybody along the ridge better start prepping to bug out. Tanner and them seem to have things under control down below, so I figured I'd ride up and pass on the news, see if y'all need a hand up here."

"Rode up, did you?" Buck asked. "I was just fixin' to turn the horses loose, and from the sound of things, you'll wanna do the same. Better that than letting 'em burn in their stalls."

The cop nodded, stoic demeanor not entirely covering the jagged anxiety beneath. He seemed painfully young, like a kid trying to be brave for an injection.

"What's your plan for the Mexicans?"

"Figured I'd just build up a firebreak around the pen, wet 'em down and pray."

I hoped he was talking about cows and not people.

"Guess that's about all you can do," the cop said.

"Tanner's got the Magnatrac," Buck said. "So we're gonna

need all hands to clear brush and get dirt moving pronto. Sage, you'd better go drag Riddle out of his bunk. Drunk or not, as long as he can hold a shovel, we can use him."

"Yes sir," Sage replied, taking the stairs two at a time.

The cop turned to me like he'd just noticed me for the first time.

"Didn't know you had company," he said. "You must be Wash's girlfriend."

I had no idea how my clever plan to escape from the online feeding frenzy and go off the grid had ended up making me more famous than ever, but here we were. I didn't answer but I didn't have to. Buck answered for me.

"Yeah, that's right," he said. "He'd been keeping the whole thing on the down low on account of her abusive ex but now…"

The lights flickered twice and then went out. The three of us stood in a silent, fire-lit tableau for a few heartbeats and the Situation did this weird slow interpretative dance inside my anxious belly. I heard the gruff rumble of a generator sputtering to life and then the lights came back on. It didn't make me feel any better.

Sage reappeared then with a rumpled and bleary-eyed Chase in tow. One curl of Chase's waxed mustache was sagging down lower than the other and his hat was on crooked. His shirt was unbuttoned, revealing a soft, hairy belly. He looked like more trouble than he was worth, but it's not like there were any other options.

"You good?" Buck asked, clearly already knowing the answer.

"I'm better than good," Chase replied. "I'm the best! Least that's what your mama told me last night."

"I'll get some coffee on," Mikayla said, appearing in the doorway dressed in practical, unisex workwear that she still managed to make look polished and expensive.

Nobody said anything. I drifted over to one of the windows, straining to see flames and figure out what was burning but the whole house had been built to face away from the road and the barn and all the other less than lovely scenery behind them. All I could see was thick yellow smoke and the flickering, feverish reflection of whatever was burning.

"I know our road is blocked," Mikayla said when she returned from the kitchen with a large mug of black coffee. "But don't you think we should start figuring how to get Angie to safety?"

"Yeah," Sage said. "Yeah, all this smoke can't be good for her and the baby. I better take her down the back way."

Mikayla shook her head, handing the coffee to Chase, who looked down at it like a child who had been given broccoli instead of ice cream.

"We need you and Brody to help build that break," she said, ignoring Chase. Brody was the cop, apparently. "I'll take Angie down on the two-up."

"She's right," Brody said. "That's the only way."

Once again, I found myself feeling like some inert but valuable object, like a briefcase full of money. Like I had no say in anything that happened to me. I didn't want to be separated from Sage and Chase, but I also didn't want to choke on smoke or die in a fire so I didn't have a ton of choices.

"Don't you worry, Angie," Sage said. "Just wait for us down in Church Creek, and I promise we'll come get you as soon as things get stabilized up here."

"Ok," I said, feeling very not ok.

"Don't you worry, darlin'," Chase said, surreptitiously doctoring his coffee with a generous splash of something from his pocket flask and toasting me like it was French champagne. "Your secrets are safe with ol' Chase."

I didn't have any idea what Chase thought he knew or didn't

know but that comment was not at all reassuring. Mikayla looked at me for a beat too long, her sunny smile sharpening in the corners.

Sage made a big dramatic show of hugging me way too hard and then grabbed one of my hands. Mikayla grabbed the other and then we were all holding hands in a little circle, ring-around-the-rosy style, with Sage asking the Lord to bless and protect me and my baby just like Wash did. I figured I wouldn't need to bother baptizing the Situation once it was born, considering all the religious benediction it had received in utero. Hell, it would probably grow up to be the Pope at this rate. Except I didn't think they were all that into the Pope at Cowboy Church.

"Amen," we all said. I knew not to cross myself that time.

"Cell tower's out." Buck tossed Mikayla a walkie-talkie. "And that front's moving fast. Y'all better get a move on."

I put on Wyman's partner's suede jacket over the nightgown, stuffed my feet into the old boots and slung my backpack over my shoulder. Once we were outside, I could hear frightened lowing and snorting as agitated bulls were mounting each other and crashing into the metal fences, casting ominous shadows across the ground.

The first thing Mikayla did was untether the cop's horse, a black-and-white female with one blue eye. The horse looked like I felt, wild and tense and ready to snap. Mikayla made a sharp sound and smacked the horse on the shoulder. The horse took off into the smoky night, and I wished she would take me with her.

Then Mikayla backed a chunky little vehicle up to where I stood. It looked like the baby brother of the monster golf cart I'd seen in Arizona. Four fat wheels and a single seat with a supportive back behind the motorcycle-style saddle seat.

"Get on," she said.

Easier said than done, but once I'd maneuvered my bulk onto the tiny seat in back, she left me on my own and ran into the barn.

I found myself looking over the controls, wondering if I could figure them out myself. I wanted to do something for myself, take my fate into my own hands in some small way. It couldn't be that hard, right?

Three more spooked horses went thundering past me, making my heart race so that when Mikayla straddled the driver's seat, I startled just like one of them.

"You ok?" she asked.

"Nope," I replied with a self-deprecating shrug.

"Well," she said. "Let's go anyway."

34.

The rocky, winding trail down the back side of the ranch was disturbingly narrow, the distance between the edge of the trail and the railing-free cliff ranging from Average Joe to Thick Vic in length. It was nowhere near enough for me to relax my death grip on the roll bar.

"Don't be scared, Angie," she yelled back over her shoulder. "I've made this trip plenty of times and never lost a rider. Yet."

"That's not very reassuring," I replied, looking away into the smoky blackness that cloaked the drop-off but didn't make it feel any safer. Shouldn't we have been wearing helmets? The only illumination was our headlights and the flickering glow of the swift moving fire reflected against the sky.

"Don't look over the edge," she scolded. "That'll just make it worse. Why don't you tell me all about your precious little baby. You got any names picked out?"

"Not yet," I said.

"Well," she said. "When are you due?"

I didn't want to tell her that I really had no idea, but that I'd just been going along with the assumption that whenever it was, it would be some time in the future. Later, next month, or the one after. Something like that. I did some half-assed math in my head, struggling to remember what the clinic nurse had told me and convert weeks to months.

"August," I said, trying to sound way more confident than I really was.

No reply for a few beats.

"August what?"

Was this a test? Was I supposed to have an exact date? Was this like some kind of normal pregnancy thing that everybody knew about but me? I should have known that avoiding learning about shit like this was going to come back to bite me.

"Third," I said, the first number that I could think of. Was that even close? What day was today? When was that day in the Mexican desert? Seemed like a hundred years ago and also yesterday.

She didn't respond for a few moments. Then, "You mean next week?"

Next week? Jesus. That couldn't be right. Could it?

"Yeah," I said.

"Let me get this straight," she said, her voice suddenly cold and drained of all the sugary charisma. "You're telling me that Guilford Arlo Washburn fucked you and filled your pussy up with live rounds early last November? That's your story?"

"I think so, why?" I asked, knowing exactly why. I couldn't believe I didn't see it sooner.

She was Wash's real redhead.

"Oh, you think so?" She slammed on the brakes, the little vehicle kicking up loose pebbles and skidding dangerously close to the edge. "You want to know what I think?"

I didn't but, as she got off of the vehicle and turned to face me, I had a feeling she was going to tell me anyway.

"I think you're a lying, scheming whore," she said, grabbing my arm hard enough to bruise and dragging me off of the back seat and onto the narrow trail.

I figured she was going to shove me over the edge at that point, but I never would have expected what she said next.

"I respect that," she said.

"Ok, look, I don't want any trouble," I said.

"Well, you got some, don't you?" she said, looking out over

the fevered landscape like some fairytale queen surveying her kingdom. "Question is, what are you gonna do about it?"

I followed her gaze across the burnt orange sky and back up the trail. The smoke was starting to sting my eyes, scouring my throat like a burnt Brillo pad. I could try to run back up to the house, but the idea of being able to outrun a woman like Mikayla would have been laughable even if I wasn't pregnant. And, even if I did, what would I say to Sage and Chase when Mikayla called my bluff?

"How can you be so sure that Wash isn't the one who knocked me up," I asked.

"I just happen to know," she said.

"He was with you, wasn't he?"

"Might have been," she said. "And I can't help but notice you ain't arguing real hard for your version of the story."

I didn't answer. I didn't have to.

Getting around her and running down the hill, away from the worst of the fire, seemed maybe slightly more possible. But then what would I do when I got to the bottom? If there were any roads down there, I couldn't see them and wouldn't know which way to go even if I could.

She pulled the walkie-talkie from her belt and thumbed the button.

"Come on through Daddy," she said, all that sugar back in her voice and then some.

"Go ahead babygirl." Buck's staticky voice popped and crackled like it was on fire too.

"We got hit by a rockslide!" She turned to me with her eyes narrowed, gaze boring into me. "Angie's hurt real bad and we need your help!"

"I'll send Chase," he said.

"Chase? That good-for-nothing drunk'll probably stumble

off the edge before he got anywhere near us. Babygirl needs her Daddy right away! Hurry…"

She tossed the walkie-talkie over the edge. The noise it made when it hit down below sounded so small, a million miles away.

"You know he's the worst fuck I ever had," she said. "Little raccoon hands grabbing at me like I'm candy and then when it's over, he always wants me to tell him how great it was."

I laughed, even though I didn't want to. I had to admit I kind of liked Mikayla.

"Now Wash," she said. "He was a soulful lover. Took it slow and looked into my eyes the whole time like he couldn't believe he got so lucky. He would have done anything for me. He loved me."

"He did," I said. "The way he talked about you, it was obvious."

"He told you about me?" She took a step closer to me. "Was that before or after you fucked him?"

"You know I didn't fuck him," I told her. "Not in November, not now."

"What did he tell you?"

"Well, not your name," I said. "Just how he felt."

"Is that right?" she said. "Did he tell you he was gonna help me kill my husband?"

35.

For a minute I just stood there, speechless. What could I have possibly said to that? All I could do was wait for her to continue.

"Guess not," she said.

"Why are you telling me this?" I asked.

"Because Wash's gone," she said. "And you're gonna help me now."

"Look," I said, backing away with my palms out, "I'm not a cop and I'm not in any position to moralize about murder. But you're on your own with whatever it is that you're planning here."

"You really think Sage and them would still help you if they knew you lied about the baby?" she asked. "I mean, you're welcome to find out, but I think you won't. Because I saw how you looked at Brody when you saw his badge and I'm willing to bet that whatever your real story is, it ain't on the right side of the law. I think you're out of options, mamacita, and if you just do like I tell you then you can walk on out of this whole mess with your cover story intact and your #GodBlessBabyWashburn hashtag unblemished."

She got on the vehicle and steered it way too close to the cliff face, so its fat tires ground against the rocky wall. A small patter of dust and stones rained down on the snub-nosed hood and she backed up and hit a second and then a third time, bringing down a more substantial clatter of jagged rocks. One more time brought down a bigger chunk of cliff the size of a filing cabinet. When it hit the trail in front of the vehicle, it broke into several pieces, effectively blocking the narrow way down.

She got a bright yellow, cylindrical emergency flashlight out of a small compartment, clicked it on and put it on the ground in the middle of the trail, pointing up the way we came.

She then backed up one last time and pulled up perilously close to the edge, jumped off, and let the little vehicle go over.

"What the fuck?" I peered over the edge and watched the vehicle bounce and spin as it fell, taking the backpack full of my meager belongings with it. "How the hell are we supposed to get anywhere now?"

The vehicle crashed hard on a lower segment of the switchback trail.

"We ain't going nowhere until we take care of some business."

"That's your business," I said. "Not mine."

"My business is your business," she replied. "Don't make me tell you again."

"What if I refuse?" I asked.

She pushed back the left side of her jacket to flash me a compact holster made of glossy cognac leather. It was not empty.

"What if I shoot you in the belly and leave you and your precious cargo to wait and see if you bleed to death before you die from smoke inhalation?"

"Right," I said, because I couldn't think of anything else to say.

"So, listen up," she said. "Here's how it's gonna go. You lay on the ground and make like you're hurt. When he bends down to check you out, I'm gonna let him have it with a rock. Once he's out, then the two of us toss him down the cliff after the two-up and we'll blame it on the slide. With the chaos of the fire and all, it'll be weeks before anyone has the spare resources to recover the body, by which time you'll be long gone."

What the fuck was I supposed to say to that? My brain kept spinning and gnawing at escape plans and options and any fucking thing other than helping to kill a decent seeming guy I barely knew. I kept coming up empty.

Meanwhile, we sat with our backs against the rock wall and waited.

"Why are you doing this?" I asked eventually.

"Why shouldn't I?" She adjusted the light. "I put up with Buck's smelly little pecker and cheerful misogyny for long enough, and now it's time for me to take my workman's comp payout and move on."

"But why kill him?" I asked. "Why not just divorce him? You could get half of his money and go anywhere you want."

"Because I don't just want half."

We were both silent for a minute.

"I have a hard time believing that you got a guy like Wash on board with killing Buck just by telling him you want money," I said.

"He spent last November here at the ranch with me while Buck was in Brazil," she said. "I let on that Buck was rough on me, just little hints at first. Eventually I let Wash think he was teasing more and more details out of me. That Buck would knock me around for not being able to give him a son like he wanted. That Wash was my only hope of ever being free and that we could be together forever if only Buck were out of the picture. Men don't do nothing to prevent each other from putting hands on women in the first place, but nothing makes their dicks harder than the fantasy that they're rescuing us from abuse after the fact. Course, I ain't telling you anything you don't already know, am I?"

For someone who had just threatened to kill me and still made sure that the butt of her gun was clearly visible in case I forgot about it, she did have some fair points.

"Buck never did hit you, did he?"

"No more than your alleged abusive ex ever hit you," she said. "But that hasn't stopped you from using that particular fairytale to get what you need. Why should I?"

I wanted to argue with her, tell her that she didn't know anything about me, but I couldn't, could I? But I also couldn't make myself feel good about participating in this murder.

I thought about Buck proudly serving me the biggest, juiciest steak. Smiling and putting his hand on my belly. Sharing that intimate, emotional moment with Sage over Wash's vest.

A moving light appeared on the trail above us, its sharp, bluish beam piercing the dancing smoke.

"Showtime," Mikayla said.

36.

When Buck came around the switchback, Mikayla threw herself into his arms.

"Oh, Daddy," she purred. "Thank God you're here, I was so scared."

I was laying on my side on the ground, tasting smoke and gritty dust in my dry mouth and feeling like I might puke or scream or maybe both. I was shaking, fists clenched too hard. I had no idea if I was going to be able to do what Mikayla asked, but it would suck to have come this far and sacrificed this much just to be taken out by a gold digger with a gun.

"Angie," he said, kneeling down beside me. "Where are you hurt?"

My heart was pounding in my bile-slick throat as I looked up at him. His pink cheeks were smudged with soot and his lank, corn silk hair was darkened with sweat and dirt. He seemed genuinely worried about me, gentle hands on my back and shoulder and I felt horrible. Horrible.

"Look out," I whispered.

I tried to stop the words, but they came out anyway, burning in my mouth like stomach acid.

"What?" He leaned closer to me, tipping one sunburned ear towards me and I wanted to scream *Behind you!* but I didn't have any more words left in me.

That's when Mikayla let him have it with the rock.

He made a weird animal noise, kind of a cross between a gasp and a grunt and hunched his shoulders like he was caught in a sudden downpour. He turned his body to face Mikayla and she hit him again, from the side this time, wide and hard and drawing blood from his temple.

He crumpled and fell across my legs. I crab-crawled backwards, desperate to get away from him, like his hot, shuddering body was contagious somehow and I couldn't stand to feel it against me. I backed myself against the rock wall and struggled to my feet while he twisted and crawled through the dirt in my approximate direction. He was still making that weird noise, rhythmically now, like panting, and it was almost funny, but it wasn't. I was pretty sure I was going to throw up, but Mikayla grabbed me and shoved the blood-slick rock into my hand.

"Your turn," she said.

I couldn't have made my numb fingers hold on to the rock if I tried. It slipped out of my grip, bounced off the toe of my boot and rolled to a stop against Buck's shoulder.

"No," I said. "No no no, I can't."

"You can," Mikayla said. "And you fucking will."

She took out the gun, finally. It was nice, clean and well maintained but all I could really see was the black hole of the muzzle.

"Pick up the rock," she said.

"Please," I said, or maybe I just thought it.

"Pick. It. Up."

I crouched down, fumbling and scrambling in the dirt like I'd gone suddenly blind while Buck clutched desperately at the sleeve of my jacket. When I finally got a grip on the rock, I got back up onto my unsteady feet.

"Muh..." Buck was saying, voice slushy and wet. "Muh..."

"Go on," Mikayla said, gesturing with her chin.

He looked up at me, blood in his hair and pale blue eyes wide. I couldn't tell if he was really seeing me or not. Then, suddenly, all I could see was Hank's face. Hank dying.

"No," I said.

"Excuse me, what?"

"You heard me," I said. "I'm not doing this. You're going to have to dispose of two bodies."

I threw the rock as hard as I could into the smoky night.

"If you shoot me," I said. "Someone will find the bullet. And if you try to push me over the edge, I'll take you with me."

"Did you forget that I know the truth about your baby?"

"No, but I don't think you're really gonna tell anyone," I said. "Because if you do, you'll have to tell them how you know."

We both just stood there, nothing left to say and no idea what to do next.

At first, I thought I was imagining it, the distant wasp-drone of a small engine and the staccato scatter of rocky dirt under fat, off-road tires. As it got louder, I realized it wasn't one engine, but two. Before I could think about the implications of this revelation, Mikayla holstered the pistol and peered over the edge as I hung as far back as I could. I don't know what she was seeing down there, but whatever it was, it shook her. She turned back to me, face pale and coldly furious.

"Hurry," she said, grabbing Buck's booted feet and yanking him toward the edge. "Come on!"

I hesitated, frozen and unable to unclench my hands. The Situation was slam-dancing like it was in a mosh pit with my heart. The engine sound was getting closer, and yesterday's steak was getting ready to hit the ejector button.

"Goddamn it," she said, letting Buck's unconscious bulk slump down against her legs. "Are you gonna help me or what? I've fucking had it with the too-good-to-get-your-hands-dirty bullshit."

"Are you kidding?" I said. "My hands are already dirtier than yours will ever be, but that doesn't mean I have to help you clean up your mess."

She let me have it then. I guess I probably deserved it.

I staggered back and sank to my knees, tasting blood. I shook my head to clear it and when I could see straight again, I saw Mikayla using her booted foot to push Buck over the edge. The meaty thud that he made when he hit the switchback below was soft and awful.

I didn't want to be anywhere near Mikayla, and I definitely didn't want to be anywhere near that crumbling, precarious edge, but I somehow found myself standing right next to both. We were both staring mesmerized at the pair of single headlights creeping upward, illuminating the stretch of the switchback just beneath the one where Buck and the ATV were blocking the path. Two vehicles, one with a single rider and one with two.

"Whoever that is," she said as they headed towards the blockage. "They'll have to turn around and go back down the way they came."

When the vehicles came upon the smashed-up ATV, the person on the first vehicle got off and walked over to toe Buck's unmoving body. I could hear some kind of exchange between him and the two on the second vehicle but couldn't make out the words.

The other driver got off the vehicle and I watched with a cold coil of dread in my chest as the two of them shoved the crashed ATV off the edge and out of their way.

"Fuck," she said as they got back on the vehicles and drove around Buck like he was an inert part of the landscape that had no bearing on whatever they were doing.

"Now what?" I asked.

"Fuck," she said again, like that was any kind of answer.

37.

It was about five minutes, maybe less before the two vehicles came up against the other side of the rock slide. I still hadn't come up with any brilliant ideas about what to do and if Mikayla had, she was keeping them to herself.

When the man who had been driving that first vehicle came clambering over the jumble of rocks, I saw that it was Ty, the skinny younger son who had been with Big Dale at the hospital. He flashed those long yellow horse teeth in a threatening smile.

"Fancy meeting you here," he said. "Where's your buddy?"

A zillion smartass comebacks shuffled through my head but somehow couldn't make my mouth cooperate.

"Huh?" I said instead.

Ty took a step closer to me, while behind him the other two riders started climbing over the rocks. These two were like discount knockoffs of his father's blond beefcake twins. Both were big, but one was thicker through the middle with a mean little mouth and hands like bulldozer blades. The other was leaner and lankier with pockmarked skin and bright, spooky meth eyes. Neither one was anybody you wanted to meet on a dangerous trail in the middle of a fiery night that had already gone nine kinds of wrong and still had plenty of room for more.

"Where's Chase Riddle?" Ty asked.

"How should I know?" I replied. "Not here, obviously."

Mikayla stepped in front of me, snapping effortlessly into the role of tearfully distraught wife.

"All I know is that my beloved husband is hurt or worse..." She paused for dramatic effect. "We need your help to get him to the hospital!"

"You got the wrong idea," he said, letting his jacket fall open to reveal a gun butt protruding, gangster-style, from the waistband of his jeans. "About who's gonna be helping who here."

Things were about to get ugly, and I seemed to be the only person without a gun.

"J.J.," Ty said to one of his thugs without taking his eyes off Mikayla. "You and Lane see about getting these rocks off the path."

"But I can't just leave Buck to die alone down there," she said, fingers creeping slowly towards the holster I knew was there.

The loud rumble and crash of one of the smaller rock fragments going over the edge made me flinch. My back was slick with cold sweat under Wyman's partner's jacket.

"This big sucker ain't gonna budge," the larger of the two thugs said—J.J., I assumed—shoulder straining against the biggest piece of the filing-cabinet-sized boulder to no avail.

"Hey, whatcha got there, little lady?" This from the other thug, Lane, who had slipped silently around behind Mikayla to press a pistol between her shoulder blades.

Mikayla narrowed her hard, turquoise eyes at Ty and raised both palms. Lane reached under her jacket and pulled her gun from its holster.

"Now normally I'd be inclined to take that kind of thing personally," Ty said as Lane handed him the gun. "But I'm gonna give you a pass seeing as you're clearly just worried about your man."

Mikayla shot me a loaded look. I had no idea if he really believed that or not, but it's not like there was anything I could do about it either way so I figured I'd better just keep my mouth shut and hope somebody other than me ended up getting shot.

I looked down over the edge. The smoke was as thick as the marine layer along the coast back in L.A. It felt like we were floating on our little chunk of trail in this vast dead void.

J.J. let out a powerlifter's guttural bellow and gave the stubborn boulder one last heroic shove. It moved about a half an inch.

"Well, shit," Ty said, pointing Mikayla's gun at her. "Guess we're walking."

38.

When we finally made it back up to the top of the trail, Ty grabbed me by the upper arm, jamming Mikayla's gun into the side of my neck.

"Now I'm only gonna ask this question one more time. Where the fuck is Chase Riddle?"

"I already told you I don't fucking know," I said, more pissed off than scared and seething with rage. "And blowing my head off won't help me remember, but honestly at this point you're welcome to give it a try. At least I won't have to deal with whatever your fucking problem is anymore."

Brody came from around the side of the barn then with his gun drawn.

"Police," he said, his anxious tenor voice trying for authority and sounding more like a high-school hall monitor. "Drop your weapon."

Both J.J. and Lane responded by pulling guns of their own and pointing them at Brody.

"Ain't you cute, piglet," Lane said with a wild, crooked grin like he was having the time of his life.

"Get your goddamn hands off of her." This from Sage who appeared out of the smoke with a fucking shotgun he got from who knows where. Because that's just how things were around these parts, apparently.

I looked over at Mikayla, the only other currently unarmed person in this macho clusterfuck. She was watching Ty like a cat watching a mouse hole, but I had no idea what she was thinking.

"We just want Riddle," Ty said, raising his voice to call out. "Riddle!"

"Ain't gonna happen," Sage replied.

"Oh it is," Ty said, moving the gun muzzle from my neck to my belly. "It's up to you if you wanna trade the life of this here baby for a cowardly piece of shit like Riddle."

"You harm Angie or that baby in any way and so help me I will fucking hunt you down..."

That was the moment when Chase came stumbling around the corner of the shop building, nearly empty whiskey bottle in one hand and his dick hanging out of his unbuttoned jeans. Not bad, on the thicker side of average but might be a grower. I had no idea what had happened to his hat.

"Can't a man answer the goddamn call of nature without..." He stopped short, body rocking like he was on the deck of a ship. "So it's like that, is it?"

"Christ, Riddle," Ty said, swinging his gun from my belly to point at Chase. "Put your fucking pecker away. Daddy wants a word with you and he don't like waiting."

"He ain't going nowhere," Sage said, taking a sliding step towards Ty and raising his aim from his center to his head. "You'll have to come through me."

"That can be arranged," Ty said, gun on Sage now.

"Hold your damn horses, will ya?" Chase turned his hips away and tucked his dick back into his jeans, buttoning only the top button and leaving the rest of the fly gaping open. "There ain't no need for this kind of Wild West theatricality. Y'all put your guns down and let's talk things over like reasonable, civilized men."

Chase staggered into the circle of fire between the five men, paused dramatically for a second as if he might be about to puke, and then belched and blew air through his rumpled mustache, stumbling sideways against J.J.

"Scuze me," he said, knees gone to rubber and half-slumping, clutching at the front of J.J.'s shirt. "Hold up a second, lemme just..."

He rested his cheek against the big man's pec as J.J. frowned at Ty over the top of his cowlicked, hatless head. Chase turned his face in my direction, those razor-sharp gray eyes going from half-mast to fully open. He winked at me.

Then he smashed the bottle into J.J.'s face.

39.

J.J. let out a surprisingly high-pitched screech and dropped to his knees, clutching the glass-studded side of his bloody face. On the way down, Chase had relieved him of his gun with a move so swift and slick that I didn't even see exactly how it happened. All I saw was that Chase was pointing that gun at Ty's head for a half a second, but then J.J. took a half-blind, bear-paw swipe at one of his legs, knocking him off balance so that when he pulled the trigger, the bullet tore Ty's jeans and raked a bloody trench into his left hip instead of hitting him in the face. Ty staggered backward, Mikayla's gun flying from his grip. It landed with a splash in a nearby livestock trough full of dirty water.

Sage lunged forward and cracked Lane in the crooked teeth with the barrel of the shotgun, causing him to drop his pistol and crumple to the dirt. Sage kicked the gun out of his reach while Brody came forward and cuffed one of his wrists. Lane reacted to this development by freaking the fuck out, shrieking and flailing his whole body like an epileptic spider monkey. He managed to nail Brody in the nuts with one of his frenetic limbs, causing the young cop to double over with a breathless grunt.

I was backpedaling away from all of this chaos and wondering what had happened to Mikayla when I heard a familiar sound I recognized from my first rodeo. A living thunderstorm of hoofs and snorts and panicked lowing, punctuated by metallic crashes and splintering wood.

Bulls. The bulls were out.

I've been in more than one near-death situation but I've never felt anything close to the pure, uncut terror that flooded my body in that moment, utterly bypassing my civilized brain. Pregnant or not, I don't think I've ever moved that fast in my life.

I was floating somewhere above all this madness, watching myself bolt away like a purse-snatcher. The fire line was creeping up the hill through the now abandoned pasture towards the barn and getting way too close for comfort. Most of the fighting cattle were barreling away down the road we came up on like a hot black river, cows and calves following the lead bulls, but a few stray bulls were still rampaging through the fenced yard between the barn and front gate, furiously slamming their heads and horns into everything around them, from hay bales and plastic buckets to vehicles. One of them found J.J. trying to get up on one wobbly knee and hooked him, sending him flying into the side of the barn like a Hollywood wire gag. I wasn't about to let that happen to me.

As I ran towards the open door to Buck's shop, I saw Mikayla straddling the livestock gate, wild hair coming loose, backlit against the dark smoke. Guns were going off all around me and I saw a dying bull that had been shot in the eye trying and failing to get back up again and again. I saw Sage climbing up the side of the dented aluminum trailer that was parked next to Wash's truck, banging his fist against the metal and yelling to get the rogue animals' attention. I didn't see exactly what happened next, but I heard a massive crash and then the trailer was on its side and sliding across the dirt like a windshield wiper until it blocked the road completely. I didn't see Sage anymore then but I couldn't afford to focus on anything but the door to the shop.

I had just barely made it inside when Lane and Ty came tumbling in behind me. Lane still had Brody's handcuff dangling from one knobby wrist as he shoved past me with his blood-splattered boss in tow. I was about to shut the door against the smoky chaos when Brody appeared with Sage across his shoulders in a fireman's carry. They were both covered in a gritty muck composed of blood and dust and fresh cow shit and Sage's right leg was obviously broken. I could see the jagged red jut of bone protruding through his torn skin.

I slammed the door.

"Anybody see Chase?" Brody asked, easing Sage down onto a pile of cowhides.

"If that motherfucker gets himself killed before I can bring him home to Daddy," Ty said between gritted teeth. "I swear to God, I'll..."

Chase threw the door open and sauntered in like he was walking into a packed arena of adoring fans.

"You'll what?" he asked with a big smart-ass grin despite the split and bleeding lip under his mustache. "You gonna dig me up and kill me again?"

"Fuck you, Riddle!" Ty said, wincing and plucking at the torn and bloody denim on his right haunch.

I leaned close to Chase. He smelled like whiskey and brush smoke.

"You ok?" I asked softly.

"Never better," he said, pulling the metal door closed and throwing the latch just as one of the terrified bulls slammed into it, denting it deeply. The latch bent but held. "Hell, I won Ada drunker than this back in '06."

"You only beat me that year because I got a bad draw," Sage replied through gritted teeth. His face was gray and slick with sweat. "I shoulda been given a re-fight."

"You still on that old horse?" Chase asked, shaking his head. He patted his pockets. "Anybody got a cigarette?"

"We got ourselves a hell of a situation here," Brody replied, kneeling beside Sage and cutting away the lower leg of his jeans around the broken bone with a pocket knife.

Nobody said anything for a tense, drawn-out minute. It still sounded like a demolition derby out in the yard, almost as loud as my heart.

Then some kind of whispered conversation started brewing between Lane and Ty, but my attention was still on Sage. Another man down because of me, but who's counting?

"Chase," Brody said. "Tell me you got a shot or two left in that hip flask."

"You bet," Chase replied as he squatted down next to Sage and held the flask to his friend's dirty lips.

"Remember when you got your oil checked in Salinas last year?" he said, holding Sage's head up and making him swallow before handing the flask to Brody. "You needed emergency surgery that night and still made it to Spanish Fork the next day."

Brody poured the rest of the contents of the flask over the gash in Sage's leg, washing the dirt and shit and clotted blood away so the protruding bone glistened pale and clean.

"Sure do," Sage replied with a shaky laugh. "This is nothing. In fact it don't hardly hurt at all!"

Brody and Sage exchanged a weighty look and I felt sick to my stomach, thinking of Thick Vic in the back of that car about a hundred years ago.

"How about this?" Brody asked, gently manipulating Sage's booted foot from left to right.

"No," Sage said, frowning.

Brody pulled up the other leg of his jeans and poked his blond-furred calf with the tip of his pocket knife.

"How about this?"

"No." Panic was stampeding through Sage's wild eyes. "No, I can't…I can't…" He gripped and twisted the hide underneath him in his sweaty fists. "I can't move my legs. I can't fucking move. I can't…"

"Ok, just take it easy," Brody was saying.

"You take it easy," Sage snapped. "I'm fucking paralyzed ain't I?"

"You don't know that," Chase said. "We're gonna get you to a doctor and see what's what but right now you gotta keep it together. You gotta be strong for Angie."

"I don't give a damn about her!" Sage said. "Don't you get it? All of this, it don't mean shit if I lose my shot to fight bulls in the NFR."

Brody was talking low and soothing to him while Chase backed off and slid over to where I stood.

"He don't mean none of that," Chase said.

I said nothing, because of fucking course he did. And why not? I was using both of them to get where I was going and it wasn't like I gave a shit about whatever the NFR was and whether or not Sage was in. There were no good guys in this fucked-up scenario. Everybody was just trying to get what they needed, an outcome that was less and less likely with each passing minute.

"I said I ain't fucking staying in here," Lane blurted out, voice suddenly twice as loud. His eyes were showing whites all the way around like Brody's frightened horse.

"Nobody's going anywhere," Brody said over his shoulder, trying to put some authority back in his quavering voice. "Until we figure out…"

"Ain't nothing to fucking figure," Lane said, eyes ping-ponging from the door to Ty and back again. "Y'all do whatever the hell you want, but I'm not…"

"Settle the fuck down, ok?" Ty raised a tense hand like he was trying to squeeze the smoky air. "Nobody's going anywhere right now."

"We need a game plan," Brody said. "We got us an injured man here."

"Fuck him and fuck you," Ty said.

"Is that all you ever say?" Brody asked.

"What ever happened to fuck me?" Chase asked. "I thought we had something special, Tyler."

"You ain't even ready for the fucking you got coming, Riddle," Ty said.

"That's what your mama said last night."

"Oh, you think this shit is fucking funny?" Ty asked. "You left my only brother to freeze to death in that walk-in so you could split with the take, so you'll excuse me if I ain't fucking laughing."

"That ain't exactly how I remember it," Chase replied. "But that don't matter anyway because you don't really give two shits about your poor dead brother, do you? In fact, I reckon you're glad he's gone, cause now maybe Daddy'll have a crumb or two of love left over for you."

Ty lunged at Chase and Brody held him back while Chase made an exaggerated come-on gesture not unlike the signal to let the bull into the arena before a fight.

"Enough already," I said, fists clenched against another swell of unhelpful fury as I wedged my sweaty bulk between them. "However big you think your dicks are, trust me I've seen bigger and couldn't care less right now anyway, so how about using your other heads for a change? Because Brody's right. We need a plan or else none of us are gonna make it out of here alive. Can't you feel how hot it's getting?"

There was a moment of shocked silence, like the dog had spoken. Like they'd all forgotten I was even there. I guess I'd been a little too successful at getting them to think of me as a helpless damsel in need of rescue.

"Damn straight," Brody said, clearly impressed.

"For starters," I said, shoving my damp hair back off my forehead. "Anybody see what happened to Mikayla?"

Brody shook his head.

"Chase?"

"I seen her open the pen to set them bulls on us," he said. "And then let the rest of the herd out just to add to the chaos. But I ain't see her since. If she's smart, she's long gone by now."

That didn't surprise me. She seemed like the only person who had been thinking strategically about this situation from the beginning. Unfortunately, I was stuck in here with a bunch of dudes who seemed more interested in trying to out-cowboy each other while being slow cooked like smoked brisket.

"Right," I said, thinking of Mikayla's gun splashing down in that water trough. "What weapons do we have? Anybody still have a gun?"

Brody held out his sidearm laying flat on his palm.

"Ain't much use without bullets."

"Anybody else?"

Everyone else shook their heads, showing empty hands.

"Ok, so shooting however many bulls are still here is out," I said. "Chase, can you get them to go somewhere else?"

"Can't say from in here," Chase responded. "Normally they'd want to follow the rest of herd rather than hang around with the likes of us but ain't nothing normal about this situation."

"There has to be a way out of this," I said. "We just need to put our heads together."

Clearly, Lane didn't agree. With near flawless comic timing, he waited a beat while we all let the seriousness of our situation sink in, and then ran for the door, wrenched it open, and high-tailed it out into the fiery night.

40.

Chase and Brody were working together to muscle the dented door closed again while Ty just stood there clenching and unclenching his hands. We couldn't see what happened to Lane, but we could hear it. Whatever it was, it was awful and went on for way too long.

Ty pulled a gun out of his waistband, pressing it into Chase's ruddy cheek. I'd been so focused on Mikayla's gun I'd forgotten all about the one he came up with.

"We're going," Ty said. "Now."

"Are you crazy?" Brody asked. "Do you not hear what's happening out there?"

"It's the best chance we have," Ty said. "Better to make a run for it while they're distracted."

"You said you didn't have a gun," Chase said with a faux-shocked expression.

"You said you'd watch out for my brother," Ty said. "Let's go."

"Tell you what," Chase said. "Lemme think it over a bit and I'll get back to you on that."

"You want me to shoot you in the fucking face?"

"I'm afraid I'm gonna have to politely decline that first invitation," Chase said. "As to the second one, I'd obviously prefer to keep my pretty face in its current configuration, thank you very much, but this ain't about me. Because Daddy ain't gonna like it if you kill me."

"He didn't say nothing about pain and suffering," Ty said. "So how about I just shoot you in the dick instead?"

"Then what?" Chase asked. "You gonna carry me home to Daddy and hope I don't bleed out before you get there?"

"Look," Brody said, showing his palms. "Nobody's shooting anybody anywhere. The only way any of us are getting out of here is if we work together."

"Shut the fuck up," Ty said, shifting the gun to point at Brody.

"Whoa," Brody said. "Easy now."

"Forget about him," Chase said. "This is between you and me, son."

Ty was sweating, thin lips peeled back over those horsey teeth and breathing way too fast. I could relate.

I was feeling a desperate, suffocating panic twisting in my chest and the Situation let me have it with a couple of karate chops just to add to the fun. I could clearly see what Ty's next move should be and was just waiting for him to realize what I already knew. He should point that gun at me. Really, that was his only move.

Chase seemed to realize this too and was trying to get Ty's focus back on him when Ty abruptly pistol-whipped Brody across the bridge of the nose, knocking the young cop to his knees.

He raised the barrel of the gun to draw a bead on Brody's sweat-slick forehead and I didn't even think twice. I just lunged forward and shoved the pegboard full of leatherworking tools with both hands. It tottered for what felt like an endless minute and then tipped over in a cascade of awls and rounded knives and chisels. From the angle that it fell, it should have hit both Ty and Chase, but Chase curved his body away and out of range with loose-jointed ease and then did a little sideways dance step to where Ty's gun had landed after spinning out of his grip.

Chase scooped up the gun while Ty struggled to his hands and knees, crawling out from under the pegboard. He was pierced all over like Saint Sebastian, awls sticking out at all angles from his bloody back and arm and there was a big, crescent shaped gash on the back of his neck. He raised a shaking palm towards Chase, but Chase wasn't joking around anymore.

His expression was grim, eyes narrow and jaw set as he raised the gun and pulled the trigger.

I flinched all over at the familiar sound, cringing and turning away with that phantom duct-tape smell burning in my nostrils, competing against the ever-present smoke from the fire. It felt like the Situation flinched too, and I hated the idea that it was learning about things like this before it was even born. I wondered if its ears were ringing too.

Little ears, Mikayla had said.

In spite of everything that she'd done, I kinda hoped she'd got away.

Ty was face down and dying under the cracked pegboard. I was grateful that his long, bloody hair was mostly covering the mess that bullet had made of his head. Chase and Brody were conferring, but it was hard to hear.

"That's on you," I think Chase was saying.

"Self-defense," Brody said. "That's the way I see it."

"Well it ain't gonna matter anyway if we don't figure a way to get the hell out of here."

"What about him?"

Both of them turned their heads back towards Sage. He was slumped on the pile of cowhides, head lolling and half-conscious.

"Can't we rig some kind of stretcher?"

Chase picked up the weird horned contraption with the single wheel.

"We could fix a couple of poles to this here dummy."

"No," Sage said softly.

"I can make a sling out of one of the hides," Brody said.

"I said no," Sage repeated. "I ain't going nowhere and there's no use pretending any different."

Chase put down the dummy and squatted down beside Sage.

"Come on now," he said, voice pitched low and soothing.

"You may be an egomaniacal Instagram princess, but I've never known you to be a quitter. Remember when Mark Olson near busted his neck in Springfield and still went back to work in the PBR? We're gonna get you to safety and taken care of and you're gonna bounce back better than ever. So maybe you don't go to the NFR this year, but there's always next year and the fans love a comeback kid!"

"I've always known you to be a bullshit artist," Sage replied, twisting the sweat-damp fabric of Chase's sooty shirt and pulling him closer. "So how about a little hard truth for a change. Truth is you can't get me out of here safely and if you waste time trying, chances are none of us are gonna make it."

"Don't talk like that," Chase said.

"You want to put your lying skills to good use," Sage said, "you tell everybody how I died a hero. Tell 'em I went out protecting Angie and saved Baby Washburn. Just leave me the gun when you go."

"Fuck no," Chase said. "No fucking way. We ain't leaving you. Tell him, Angel!"

Angel. I frowned, cold suddenly despite the stifling, smoky heat.

41.

"My name's Angie," I said.

"Course it is," Chase said, backpedaling. "I was just being poetic is all."

"Right," I said.

Chase never did say what secret he thought he knew about me, but he clearly knew who I really was. Or did he? I looked over at Brody to see if he recognized me too, but his expression was stoic and gave me nothing to go on.

"Are the keys in Wash's truck?" I asked instead of screaming. I figured I could scream later, after hopefully not dying in this tool-filled oven.

"Yup," Chase said.

"You think you can get to it?"

"Sure." He didn't sound so sure. "No problem."

"Well, you said that bulls wanna be with other cattle more than they want to be with us, right?"

"Some of them are just ornery and love to fuck with you, but generally speaking, yeah."

"So the reason these bulls are still up here is because they're stuck here just like we are," I said. "If you can get the truck started maybe you can push that trailer out of the way so they can follow the others."

"That's a damn good idea, Angie," Chase replied, hitting my fake name a little too hard, overcompensating. "I swear we're gonna make a hand outta you yet!"

Brody pointed up to the large industrial fan built into the wall, high up near the peak of the roof.

"Why don't you climb up there and see if you can get the lay of the land?"

The two of them carried a ladder over to where the fan was and Chase climbed up to peer out between the rusted blades.

"Looks like we got three bulls left alive in the yard," he said. "One of them is hung up in a busted fence over on the barn side but the other two are free and looking for trouble. That trailer's blocking 'em in now, but Angie's right." He started climbing back down the ladder. "If I can just get that out of the way, it'll be a cinch to drive 'em down that road."

"Right, ok," Brody said, taking Chase's place on the ladder. "Lemme see if I can make some noise and provide a little distraction to get you a head start." He started banging on the fan grate. "Hey! Up here, you miserable sons of bitches! Up here!"

Chase nodded at me, an uncharacteristically serious expression on his red, sweaty face. Then he slipped out the door without another word.

"They ain't listening!" Brody said, a series of crashes nearly drowning out his voice. "Holy smokes, I think Lane is still alive."

"Can you see Chase?" I asked, fingers clasped tight on my belly and feeling like I was trying to follow a boxing match on a neighbor's radio.

"Nah he…Wait a second…Oh man…"

"That's not fucking helpful!" I said, anxious frustration welling up in my hot, scratchy throat. "What the hell is going on out there?"

"He's up on the fence now," Brody said. "Dang that was close."

"Did he make it to the truck?"

"Not yet, not yet, wait…"

"Oh my god," I said. "You are officially the world's worst sportscaster. Get down and let me look."

“I don’t know if that’s a good idea,” he said, wide eyes still riveted on whatever was happening in the yard.

“I don’t know if it’d be a good idea to punch a cop in the nuts either, but I’m gonna start seriously considering it if you don’t get down off that fucking ladder.”

“Wow, ok,” he said, making his way down the ladder. “Jeez.”

I shoved him out of the way and started working my way up the ladder with my stomach turned to one side. It actually wasn’t a good idea at all, but I was committed and not about to admit I’d been wrong.

By the time I got high enough to see, Chase had made it to the truck and was gunning the engine.

“He’s in!” I said.

One of the terrified bulls slammed into the back panel of the truck, skewing it hard but somehow Chase was able to keep control of the vehicle and start pushing the front bumper into the crumpled trailer.

“I think he’s got it now,” I said.

“Well then you better come down from there and help me get this stretcher rigged,” he said. “We need to be ready to move Sage as soon as possible.”

I looked back out over the mayhem in the yard. Chase had backed up and slammed into the trailer again, shoving it further out of the way. I hadn’t noticed Lane before, but I saw him then and wished I hadn’t. He was still alive. Barely.

I took a long slow breath and then backed slowly down the ladder.

We had been working quickly and silently for several minutes, lashing the poles to that single wheeled cart to form a makeshift stretcher that worked like a wheelbarrow, when Brody finally spoke up.

“Look,” he said. “I appreciate you saving my life and all.”

Silence played out and I could feel the weight of the other half of that sentence hanging in the smoky air between us.

"But?" I finally said.

"But you know I'm gonna have to turn you in."

"What?" I clenched my fists. "Why?"

"Because I'm a lawman," he said. "First and foremost. That doesn't mean anything if I don't follow the law."

A lawman. That was about right. All the corrupt cops in all the world and I end up with Dudley fucking Do-Right.

"You were willing to let Chase off the hook on a claim of self-defense," I said. "What do you think happened between me and that cop? You think I just randomly decided to shoot her in cold blood for no reason? She was shooting at me!"

"That's up to a jury to decide," he said.

"But what about Corbin?" I asked, trying not to let panic twist my voice. "If you turn me in, he'll find me and you know as well as I do that he's not gonna wait for a jury verdict."

He paused for a moment, frowning.

"Look I know that man ain't right," he said. "We all supported him in the beginning out of sympathy and respect for a fallen officer, but he's gone way too far with all this YouTube crazy talk about vengeance and wanting to look in your eyes while he watches you die."

"Then let me go," I said. "Let me walk away and you'll never see or hear from me again."

"Can't do that," he said. "Justice is justice and I don't get a say in the matter."

"Well, I guess you'll do what you feel you have to do," I said. "But it won't make any difference if we all burn to death up here, so how about we focus on surviving long enough to continue this complex moral debate another day?"

"Right," he said.

Chase reappeared in the doorway then.

"Come on," he said. "Time to make like horse shit and hit the trail!"

"Ok," Brody said. "Ok."

I had no idea where things stood between us, but didn't have time to think too deeply about it.

"No no no," Sage was saying as Brody and Chase lifted the blood-soaked hide and him with it. "Just leave me."

"No can do," Chase said, strapping Sage into the stretcher. "Your mama won't be so generous with her formidable and widely lauded charms if I fail to save your sorry ass."

Chase's corny and compulsive jokes about everybody's mama were starting to take on an anxious, almost desperate tenor. Sage wasn't laughing. He didn't seem entirely coherent and he grabbed repeatedly at my wrist with weak, clammy fingers. I had this weirdly vivid sense-memory of holding Wash's hand, almost like a double exposure or a ghost. My life just kept on folding in on itself, xeroxing itself into ever-degrading copies of copies.

"Pray with me, Angie," he said. "We need to pray."

"Um..." I looked up at Chase, not knowing what to say. "I..."

"God'll just have to hold the line," Chase said. "Because that fire won't wait."

We got the contraption out through the door after some awkward maneuvering. The bulls were gone and the mesmerizing line of fire was just on the other side of the open gate. Shimmering heat and black smoke filled the air and it was getting harder and harder to breathe.

"Which way?" Brody asked. "Maybe we can..."

Whatever he was about to say got blown out the back of his head, along with the rest of the contents of his skull.

42.

There was Mikayla, holding a rifle and looking like a million bucks despite the soot and heat and chaos. Looking like her Ralph Lauren fashion campaign had been commandeered by Sam Peckinpah. Looking the way I wished I looked, instead of how I really looked. Probably the way you wish I looked too, honestly.

But none of that mattered because she looked like the last thing I was gonna see before I ate a bullet of my own.

The gun went off at the same time as Chase slammed into me like a bull, knocking me sideways and landing on top of me, forcing all the breath out of my body in an unlovely grunt.

Another shot pinged off metal way too close to my head and when I looked up between my dirty fingers, I saw that Chase had us wedged behind the humpbacked bulk of some kind of tractor.

"Angie?" Mikayla called. "Why don't you come on out of there?"

"Why?" I asked. "So it'll be easier to shoot me?"

"I'm not looking to shoot you," she said. "After all, us girls gotta stick together, don't we?"

Chase crawled off of me and got up into a low crouch with his back against the shop wall.

"Keep her talking," he whispered, making a rolling gesture with his index finger.

I nodded and he started swiftly creeping away from Mikayla and around the back side of the shop.

"Why should I trust you?" I asked. "How do I know you won't just kill me the first chance you get?"

"Because we got us a unique opportunity here," she replied. I couldn't see where she was, but her voice sounded closer. "Don't you see? A couple of poor defenseless females, innocent victims caught in the crossfire between desperate criminals. Nobody ever needs to know what happened to Buck or who the father of your baby really is. Nobody will question our version of events and we'll both walk away scot-free."

"What about Chase?" I asked.

"What about him?"

"Can't you just let him go?"

Her voice seemed even closer now, almost right on the other side of the tractor. The fire line was getting closer too, smoke scouring my aching lungs.

"What do you care what happens to a drunken coward like him?" she asked. "You think he gives a damn about you? He's proven time and time again that he don't care about anyone but himself. Ain't that right, Riddle?"

Where was Chase? He seemed like he had a plan when he started making his way around the back of the shop, but maybe he just took off and left me here as a decoy. Maybe he really didn't care about anyone but himself. Either way, if he didn't answer her she was gonna realize that he was no longer behind the tractor with me and then who knew what might happen.

A rough, slurry voice that wasn't Chase's called out across the yard.

"Mikayla!"

A familiar voice, for all its roughness.

Buck.

Buck was still alive.

I couldn't resist peeking out from behind the tractor's flank just in time to see Chase tackle Mikayla from the left side. Meanwhile, Buck was over by the trail head, doing a slump-shouldered zombie shuffle towards the skirmish. His pale hair was stiff with clotted blood, hands reaching and clutching at the smoky air.

"Mikayla!" Buck called again. "Mikayla, where you at? Musta hit my head and I can't hardly see! Mikayla!"

Mikayla didn't go down under Chase's weight and the two of them were grappling furiously over possession of the rifle. My money was on Mikayla.

I needed to change those odds.

I struggled to get my feet under me, feeling a cold surge of adrenaline laced with metallic nausea. Chase was my only hope of finding Harlan. I had to do something. There was a fat, burrito-sized chunk of white rock that had been set behind one of the rear tires on the tractor to keep it from rolling away. It was almost too heavy to pick up with one hand, but I managed.

Buck was still calling out for Mikayla while she was hissing and spitting with her attention totally locked on Chase. Chase's eyes flicked to me and he gave an almost imperceptible nod and then shoved Mikayla away as hard as he could.

She staggered backwards, left arm pinwheeling wildly while holding the rifle close to her body with the right.

"Mikayla," I said, not nearly as loud as Buck but loud enough to make her turn her head towards me.

That's when I let her have it with the rock.

She went down quicker and harder than Buck had, first to her knees and then flat on her face in the dirt with the rifle trapped beneath her. I figured I should make sure and finish the job, so I hit her again and then a third time.

Chase took my arm and held me gently back from a fourth blow. I was too tired to fight him so I just let the bloody rock drop to the ground beside Mikayla and we backed away together.

Buck was still calling her name as he blindly zig-zagged through the yard.

By the time we got back over to the makeshift cart we'd

made to haul Sage out of there, it was too late. I couldn't tell if he'd gotten shot by Mikayla or just died of his injuries. I didn't want to look too closely at him. I didn't want to look at Brody's body either, so I just stared into the shimmering orange curtain of the encroaching fire line while Chase had a little breakdown over Sage.

He was clutching at Sage's shirt, swearing, sobbing and coughing with snot running down his chin and tears making clean tracks through the soot on his cheeks. Meanwhile, Buck finally found Mikayla and was on his knees clutching her to his chest and wailing with his face turned up to the smoldering sky.

I was the only one who wasn't crying.

43.

I had no idea how long we had been walking. I could see the main line of fire to our right, snaking away down the hill, but the smoke had gotten so thick that I could no longer see the cliff edge. I was coughing non-stop, rubbing my sore, gritty eyes. Maybe the sun was coming up, or maybe it was just the fire burning brighter, hotter, closer.

It had taken some doing to convince Chase to leave Sage's body at the ranch. He had this notion that he needed to make sure his friend got a proper burial, but it was becoming increasingly clear that trying to drag that cart with us would only slow us down and possibly leave all three of us without a proper burial.

Even though he claimed he didn't go in for church-type stuff, Chase had wanted to say a prayer for Sage before leaving. Turned out he was too choked up to speak, so I went ahead and recited the one I knew. The one about Mary, a mother like I was, praying for us in the hour of our deaths just like I was doing for yet another man who had died because of me. I felt trapped in a maze of echoes.

I guess that old prayer was good enough because Chase nodded his head and said amen along with me at the end. Nothing miraculous or spiritually significant happened then and we both knew that the hour of our deaths was gonna be sooner rather than later if we didn't get the hell out of there, so we did.

We followed the narrow slice of rocky dirt between the cliff's edge and the fenced pasture. It wasn't exactly the safest route, but it was the only way out that wasn't blocked by flames.

Sometimes we held hands without really knowing why.

At one point we passed a lone, unsteady calf wandering aimlessly along the fence line and mooing pitifully, black soot crusted around its pink nostrils. I wondered if it was the same calf whose mother wanted to kick my ass when we first arrived at the ranch. Was she dead? Had she run off with the rest of the herd? Either way it was hard not to take that as a bad omen. There was nothing we could do to help the lost calf, so we just kept on walking.

The sky eventually turned a dirty, sulfuric yellow and the wind picked up a bit so I was able to make out a little more of the nightmare landscape around us. We were able to turn away from the cliff's edge, cutting through a blackened field and onto flatter ground. We picked our careful way between flat gray rectangles that probably used to be structures of some kind and blackened scraps of busted farm equipment sticking up from the ash like dinosaur bones. We had to detour around husks of burnt-out vehicles and a dead horse. We didn't see any other humans.

It was about an hour later when we found the jeep.

It was red and covered with soot and ash that almost obscured the volunteer firefighters' logo on the open driver's side door. Most importantly, it was running. No sign of the owner.

"You ok to drive?" I asked Chase as he climbed in behind the wheel.

"Hell," he said. "If the last six hours haven't sobered me the fuck up, then I don't know what will. Get in."

He had a point. Anyway, I wasn't in any kind of shape to be driving myself. I got in.

Inside the jeep smelled clean and dirty at the same time, like a laundromat in a crummy neighborhood. There wasn't a lot of clutter, just a stiff, navy blue canvas jacket that had been carelessly tossed across the passenger seat. It featured the same firefighter logo as the one on the door. I draped it over my exhausted body like a blanket and hunkered down against the window as Chase pulled out in a plume of ashy dust.

We were mostly silent except for coughing for a long time, bumping cautiously along a series of rough, unpaved roads. We passed through forests of blackened trees like burnt matchsticks and swerved around dead and dying cattle. We saw a man sifting morosely through the ruins of his house and two women tending to a burned dog. Not one of them looked up as we passed.

We eventually hit some real tarmac and I was starting to feel a little drowsy when out of nowhere, Chase spoke up.

"Well," he said. "Guess we might as well come clean."

"About what?" I asked, even though I was pretty sure I already knew.

"I reckon you want to know what really happened with Little Dale," he said. "And I'd sure like to know exactly what happened between you and Wash and the law and whoever the fuck else was involved in what you got going on in there."

I honestly couldn't have cared less about what happened to Little Dale. It's not like there was anything I could do differently if I decided that Chase really was no good and I already knew that I was no good. We were stuck with each other now regardless, but he clearly needed to talk and it gave me something to concentrate on other than the hellscape around us or my aching back and hips.

"You heard of Hezzie's BBQ?" Chase asked.

I shook my head.

"It's a family affair. Got roadside stands all through East Texas and Louisiana and one or the other of them boys is always winning some TV contest or chili cook-off. They got fuck-you money from way back is what I'm saying. Anyway, ol Hezzie's granddaughter Lula Rae Hook decided she was sick of cooking 'em and wanted to start breeding 'em instead. Got her a degree in AgSci and got into bucking stock, which is how she wound up going head-to-head with Big Dale over them Bad Day straws."

Up ahead in the road there was a cluster of other fire vehicles. Chase pulled a hard left to detour around them without interrupting the flow of his story.

"Big Dale found out that she had temporarily hidden the goods inside a walk-in freezer in their Nacogdoches kitchen. It was past midnight when we let ourselves in, and still hotter than Satan's taint. It actually felt kinda good being inside that freezer at first, but it wound up taking us way too long to find the tank. We looked and looked and had just about half froze ourselves by then but no dice. What we were looking for was a portable semen tank. That'd be a metal canister about yea big."

Chase nudged the wheel with his knee while using his hands to indicate a fat, phallic shape about 17 inches long. I felt like I should crack some kind of joke about that, but couldn't quite string the words together in the right order, so I just nodded.

"But Lula Rae knew we'd be looking," he continued, hands back on the wheel. "So she wasn't gonna leave it out for us to grab and go. Turned out she had it stashed inside a bin marked 'off cuts,' buried underneath a bunch of plastic-wrapped I don't know what. Ears and assholes, I reckon."

I could still smell charred, dead livestock all around us and had to clench my teeth against a wave of greasy nausea. I was really starting to see the appeal of going vegan. Chase continued unabated, in full hyperbolic storyteller mode now.

"We got the tank dug out of that bin and were fixin' to get the fuck out when a couple of Lula's boys showed up shooting. Well, I did what any man would do when faced with the undeniable fragility of our brief human existence. I shot back.

"Little Dale managed to shoot the shit out of a tub of Blue Bell buttered pecan ice cream minding its own business on the top shelf, but it was me that took care of them two boys. One went down right away, but the second one still had enough spunk left in him to shoot Little Dale in the belly before stumbling out of the freezer, locking us in, and then dying against the damn door for good measure."

He paused like he was feeling out his audience, looking for a reaction from me to keep the momentum going.

"Fuck," was all I could manage.

"Fuck is about right," he said. "I was so cold by then I thought my teeth was gonna chatter right out of my head, but I somehow managed to pry the bottom hinge off that door. Top one was rusted solid and so my only half-assed hope of escape was to push that bottom part of the heavy door out as far as it could go with a dead man slumped up against it and somehow squeeze through that itty bitty wedge of space between the door and the frame.

"Well, you know, I always have been good at wriggling out of a tight spot, so I shoved the tank out first and followed it forthwith. Little Dale on the other hand, well he wasn't all that little, even if he wasn't gutshot and screaming like a strung-up hog. There was no way to get him out of there without opening the door all the way."

Chase trailed off for a minute, chewing at that by now ragged and soot-blackened mustache with his gaze locked on the horizon. We were finally starting to put the worst of the smoke behind us. Up ahead in the distance was a sharp slice of blue sky.

"I've told a lot of different versions of this story," Chase said. "To myself and to anybody who'd listen, but none of them are the whole truth. I told myself there were probably more guns on the way and that I didn't have time to fuck around getting that body out of the way of the door, figuring how to get it all the way open while it was half off its hinges, or dragging Little Dale's not-so-little ass out of that freezer, and I suppose that could have been the case. Or maybe not. But the real truth is that I didn't stick around to find out. Not because I couldn't, but because I didn't want to."

More silence then. The blue sky was getting closer.

"But you took the semen," I said. "Didn't you?"

"Sure did."

"What happened to it?"

"Sold it for half of what it was worth and blew every penny in one weekend. Ain't never been one for saving. Big Dale has been making all this noise about how he wants to avenge his firstborn and all that, but what he really wants is to punish me for letting someone other than him have them straws."

"I can't imagine he'll be thrilled when he finds out about his second-born," I said.

"Don't reckon he will," he said.

Chase started coughing then, deep and rough and hunched over the wheel with the intensity of it. He rolled down the window and spit a thick wad of black gunk out into the slip-stream.

"So," Chase said after the coughing fit settled down. "I guess the long and short of it is this. You're not the only one who needs to go off the grid."

I didn't know how to feel about that, but I was too exhausted to come up with any kind of cogent response so I just made a sort of affirmative noise and looked away out my window. I still needed him to help me find my way to Harlan's, obviously, and I can't say that I was unhappy to learn that he now had his own selfish reasons to do it. All I could do was wait and see how it all played out.

I thought we'd been in Utah that whole time, but I then saw a sign welcoming us to the Beehive State, so I guess we must have been in Wyoming. That shit about beehives seemed made up, like why wasn't it the Salt Lake State? Anyway my grade school geography was admittedly a little sketchy even at the best of times, especially when it came to all those big blocky states between Illinois and California.

Chase didn't start bugging me for my story until we hit Idaho.

"Come on now, Angel," he said. "I showed you mine for real this time, didn't I? Warts and all."

I was exhausted and raw and utterly sick of lies, so I told him the truth. Every fucking bit of it.

44.

We'd been driving so long, I felt like there was no reality outside this jeep. Like we were trapped in here together forever. We stopped for gas and snacks only when we absolutely had to. I pissed on the side of the road. We talked about trying to switch cars, but it seemed too risky. I offered to take turns driving, but Chase refused.

"I'm good," he said.

"Neither one of us is good," I said.

"You got that right," he said, getting back behind the wheel.

Eventually I drifted off with the firefighter's coat pulled up under my chin and my aching head against the cool glass. I had no idea how long I'd been out when Chase shook my arm, jolting me out of another fucked up duct-tape dream.

"Heads up," he said. "We got a problem."

There was a cop car following us.

"Shit," I said. "Where are we?"

"Just north of Conconully," he said. "Nearly there."

I looked around. There was nothing but trees all around us. No other cars. Just us and the cop car.

Chase sped up and the cop car sped up. He slowed and so did they. This wasn't good.

"You might want to put your seat belt on right about now," Chase said.

I'd left it off while snoozing to avoid squashing my belly and tits but he didn't have to tell me twice. Eying our pursuer in the rearview, I buckled up with shaky fingers, nerves jangling. The Situation kicked out against the restraint.

Without warning, Chase veered into the oncoming traffic lane, slammed on the brakes and then gunned it in reverse. The cop car shot past us while Chase pulled an extravagant U-turn and then took a hairpin right onto a private dirt road with a rusted chain across it. The chain snapped and dangled from the Jeep's grill guard like Christmas tinsel.

The cop car had its siren going now but I couldn't see it through the thick woods and all the dust we were kicking up. Driving that fast on rough terrain had to be a bad idea, but I didn't have any other clever alternatives to suggest so I just kept my mouth shut and hung on.

I could see the police lights flashing through the trees then, getting closer and closer and started wondering if dying in a crash would be better or worse than going to jail. That was when some crucial part of the Jeep failed spectacularly, sending us careening sideways into a rocky ditch.

I was more than a little dazed, and seemed to be having trouble with the buckle on my seatbelt when Chase tore the passenger side door open and hauled me out of the Jeep. I hadn't even seen him get out.

"Go," he said, giving me a hard shove. "Head due north and I'll be right behind you."

I had no idea which way was north but assumed that he meant the direction that he'd pushed me. I put my arms into the sleeves of the firefighter's coat, pulled it tight around my neck and did the closest thing to running that I could manage, plunging into the thick underbrush.

Branches clawed at me and tugged at the dirty hem of the nightgown as I pushed my way through the dense tangle into a section of woods that seemed to be slightly less overgrown. The area between the tall, mossy pine trees was mostly knee-high ferns and lichen-draped branches over a nearly solid ground cover of rusty brown fallen needles and slick dead leaves. It didn't smell piney and fresh like I had imagined, like that cleanser my mom used to use. It smelled sweetly rotten and loamy, like wet dirt and old bones.

There wasn't going to be any running through this rough terrain, but I picked my crooked way between the ferns as quickly as I could. I could hear shouts from the road, and then the crack of a shot echoing through the trees. That was all the inspiration I needed to push myself harder, to speed the fuck up and get as far away from whatever was happening back there as possible.

When the cold flush of adrenaline started to wear off, I noticed how hard it was to catch my breath. I felt woozy and lightheaded and remembered Chase's warning about the altitude where we were going, how I should take it slow at first because it might take time for me to acclimate. So much for that plan.

I pushed grimly onward, telling myself Chase would be right behind me. That all I had to do was hang on until he caught up with me and he would know the right way to go.

I thought I'd read something as a kid about moss growing on the north side of trees, but the ancient trees around me were furred green on all sides, all different types of moss that reminded me of scraggly trailing hair and lacy gray doilies and plush green AstroTurf. Not to mention all the frilled fungi laddering up the trunks like elf shelving. None of them seemed to favor any one side over another.

I was sick to death of having to rely on other people to save my double-wide ass. I was a multiple murderer on the run from the law, not some damsel, but I couldn't shake this deep-seated primal fear of being a hopeless city girl lost and alone in this vast and unforgiving forest.

I forced myself to keep sharp, to pay attention. I tried to notice the direction of the sunlight and guess which way was north based on that. I tried not to notice how low the sun was sinking or think about how soon it would be dark.

After a seemingly endless slog through undifferentiated woods, I stumbled on something that looked like a crooked trail. Maybe just a pathway trampled by passing deer and it didn't go exactly in the direction I'd guessed was north, but it was close enough and it was way easier than high-stepping through ferns and jagged broken branches. I was having to stop more often than I liked to catch my breath, but I was putting more and more distance between me and whatever was happening on the road. I was feeling pretty proud of myself until I fell.

The trail had been winding slightly uphill for about thirty minutes and then took a dramatic downward turn. It wasn't actively raining, but there was a cold, clingy mist drifting between the trees and everything was suddenly much wetter than it had been. The slimy dead leaves under the smooth soles of my cowboy boots caused me to slip hard to the left and I tried to steady myself against a tree trunk, but the mossy trunk was also treacherously slippery. I wound up sliding awkwardly down a bank on my ass and slamming sideways into a fallen log.

The wet, spongy wood disintegrated in my hands as I tried to haul myself up, dumping a scatter of startled insects down the front of my nightgown. As I crab-crawled backwards, frantically brushing bugs off my painfully swollen tits, I was hit with a sharp spasm of lower back pain.

I froze, breathless and stunned by the staggering enormity of the pain. When I say it felt like getting shot, keep in mind that I've been shot so I'm not just falling back on hyperbolic metaphor.

It figured I'd throw my back out hundreds of miles from the

nearest chiropractor. Carrying the Situation around for as long as I had, it was kind of surprising that it hadn't happened sooner.

It seemed to subside for a moment, and I was able to get myself back up to my feet before it hit again, this time seeming to permeate my entire lower body, and I suddenly felt something weighty and slick slide loose from inside me and fill the crotch of my rumpled, muddy panties.

How could I have been so stupid? I wasn't having back spasms. I was having a baby.

45.

Gazing with paralytic dread at the thing in my dropped panties, I wondered if it was a piece of the Situation. But it didn't look like a human body part, it was soft and gooey and looked like a dead albino salamander trapped in a bloody Jell-O shot. When I dumped it out onto the carpet of wet needles, it splattered into a sticky puddle.

Whatever it was, I was in trouble.

I had to keep moving no matter what. It would be dark soon and I couldn't let myself dwell on that, so I pulled my panties back up over my mud-frosted thighs and forced myself to put one foot in front of the other.

It had to be way too early for this to be happening, didn't it? My mind kept on going back to that clinic and the friendly nurse with the pink leopard glasses, the one who told me I was twenty-eight weeks pregnant. When had that been? Was that May? June?

I remembered the cheesy decorations for Cinco de Mayo at the clinic and as I counted carefully, laboriously forward from that week, I realized with horror that it wasn't too early for this at all. In fact, I was right on time and maybe even a little bit late. I was lucky it didn't happen while I was fighting with Mikayla about when it was supposed to happen. Or during either of the murders that I committed last week.

How had I allowed myself to lose track of time so completely? All my preggo fetish clients had insisted that I didn't look big enough to be more than six months in and I guess maybe I had started to believe them. It was much easier than reckoning with the inevitable.

Another back spasm hit, knocking me stumbling against a tree trunk, digging my icy fingers into the ancient grooves in the bark. I couldn't stop. I kept walking.

I'm not going to go into the gory details here because it's like rodeo. If you already know, you don't need me to explain and if you don't, well you really don't want to know. Suffice to say that I found myself desperately in need of a toilet, only of course there wasn't one and nothing to wipe myself with either. But even after I thought I'd gotten that humiliation over with and threw away my now utterly unspeakable underwear, I still kept on feeling like I needed to go more. Nobody tells you how much having a baby is like shitting.

To be fair, it's not like I had been asking.

I felt furious at my former self for putting off looking at any information about what was happening to my body. I'd put all my faith into some imaginary fantasy of Winnie the Midwife, who currently seemed about as realistic as Winnie the fucking Pooh. How did I let myself become so helpless? So dependent on others? I wanted to blame the hormones, but it was really just me. I was broken inside, a shameful shadow of who I used to be.

Suddenly, the idea that Chase was coming to save me was utterly laughable. Chase, the man who left his partner to die over a cooler full of jizz. Everyone who cared about me was dead. There was only me and the person that the Situation would turn out to be, if it survived. If I survived.

I had a little bit of a reprieve from pain right around the time I realized that the light was fading fast, and it was getting cold. Born-again L.A. woman that I was, I thought of late July nights as balmy and mild, cooler than the sunny days but never too cold to fuck in a convertible. But, like Dorothy by way of Angelyne, I was so not in L.A. anymore.

I felt around in the pockets of the firefighter's coat. Cigarettes, lighter, keys, and a cherry cough drop. In addition to keys, the chunky black ring had a flashlight the size of my pinkie and a mini Leatherman tool.

I was starting to get awfully thirsty, and like so many of the things about my situation and the Situation, I really didn't want to think about that too hard. I unwrapped the cough drop and popped it into my mouth, carefully folding and saving the little wrapper because I'm a killer but not a litterbug. The cough drop tasted harsh and medicinal on my parched tongue, but it made my mouth water. Which wasn't anything like real water, but it would have to do.

I decided to save the batteries in the little flashlight and not turn it on until I absolutely needed it. In the back of my mind, I kept on telling myself that I would get somewhere safe or that, if not Chase, then someone else would find me before it got really dark.

Turns out I absolutely needed that flashlight way sooner than I had hoped.

When you think about the word dark, you have ideas in your head of what that means to you. To me it meant nighttime in my childhood bedroom, with sharp shadows dancing on the ceiling and a faint streetlight glow squeezing around the edges of my scratchy old purple plaid curtains. It meant crouching behind heavily perfumed dresses in the musty back of Nonna Vincenza's closet playing hide-and-seek with only a sliver of light under the sliding mirrored doors. It meant desert nights on the road, sky full of stars and passing truck headlights and maybe that's the fevered neon of Vegas in the distance or maybe just my imagination.

That wasn't really dark.

No matter what happened to me in my life up until then, I

had never really been that far from some kind of light source. Even when the power went out in my house in the Valley, there was still a cell phone or my laptop or a scented candle by my bed or even just the ambient glow of the river of headlights on the freeway reflected back down to earth by the ever-present layer of smog.

But here, as the sun took a sudden suicide plunge into twilight behind the unseen bulk of jagged mountains, darkness snuggled up to me and made itself at home. No pretty show of warm sunset colors that night, just this grim leaching away of color from everything around me that felt like going blind. Whatever stars may have existed beyond the treetop canopy were hidden from me.

Birds were noisily letting everybody know that darkness had arrived, chirping like newsboys excited to share a terrifying headline before falling ominously silent. Bugs were everywhere, attracted to my labored breathing and to the sticky gunk on my thighs. It was hard to tell their bites from the itchy lashes of nettles and underbrush.

I turned on the little flashlight right at the moment that another breathtaking wave of pain smashed into me like Jaws trying to bust up the Orca. It was as if the pain had been attracted to the light. I almost dropped the key ring as I leaned against a tree, gritting my teeth against a sound that didn't even seem human.

I knew I was in deep shit, just like I had known these past few months that I was going to have a baby. I just didn't want to think about it. I shoved the knowing down and away and concentrated on taking each slippery step without falling on my ass. On breathing through another wave of pain. On surviving for ten seconds, and then ten more.

The cherry cough drop was long gone, and I was going to

need to find some water somewhere soon. It wasn't exactly raining, just wet. Like the air itself was wet, full of suspended droplets that were just big enough to soak me to the bone but not big enough to drink. I kept on thinking I could hear a faint, distant trickle like water flowing over stones, but it never seemed to get any closer. I couldn't keep on blundering through the woods in the dark, possibly getting farther and farther from where anyone could find me. Anyone human anyway.

That was not a fun thought. Surely there had to be animals around up here, and not the cute Disney kind, frolicking with butterflies and waiting to help the poor lost princess. Hungry, desperate animals trying to stay ahead of the long, hard winter and angling for any easy score that might give them a little more fat to tide them over until the spring. Weighing the chances of their cubs surviving over mine.

Pain again, and the killing thirst digging deeper into my raw and ragged throat. I was having a harder and harder time stifling my screams.

I had to find that water. It couldn't be far, but I was having more and more trouble catching my breath and kept feeling like I was going to pass out. I kept thinking about that pineapple pop the buckle bunnies gave me back in Arizona, how cold and good it was and how I'd chew my own leg off to get another one.

The pencil-thin, blueish beam from the flashlight made the darkness around me seem much darker, if that was even possible. It was like I was moving through a black void, following a fleeting hubcap-sized circle of reality. I became hyper-aware of sounds, like the thick slushy drag of my boots through the rotten leaves and the crackle of brush that I trampled and shoved aside and bulldozed my way through, all backed up by the sound of my tortured breathing. And somewhere up ahead and to the left, that teasing promise of water.

I found myself thinking of Cody, unwitting co-creator of the Situation. I thought about the little flashlight he had on his key-chain, almost identical to this one. I thought about walking down a dark desert road with him the night we met, following that meager beam of light into a future neither one of us could imagine. I thought about watching him die. I thought about giving up and joining him.

But I couldn't. I had to quit thinking and keep moving.

I thought I was doing a great job of not thinking about how fucked I was, until I saw a glistening puddle beneath some crushed ferns and shined the light directly on it. It took me a second to realize what it was, but when I did, I felt this crushing hopelessness grip my heart in its cold fist.

It was the remains of the weird, gooey salamander I'd shaken out of my panties several hours ago.

I was walking in circles.

I sank to my knees, my whole body feeling frozen like I was already dead. There was no point in going on.

46.

I didn't die though, and I can't say that I was particularly happy about that fact at the time. What happened instead was that this huge gush of fluid came out of me and even I knew that had to be my water breaking. I figured that meant the baby was coming out right then and there, but it turns out this whole giving birth thing actually takes way longer than it does in the movies.

I paced around when I could, tramping down the brush in a crooked figure eight shape. I tried licking water off of some leaves, which tasted like shit and just made me even more thirsty. It wasn't like it was Chicago cold or anything, but it was way too cold to be running around in the woods at night with no underpants. The wind in the pine trees sounded like tires on wet asphalt, filling me with irrational bursts of hope that somehow a car was coming, even though I was miles away from anything resembling a road. I alternated between feeling like I was going to pass out and feeling like I was going to have a heart attack, all the while feeling like my hip bones were being pried apart with hot tongs. I tried to see myself from outside my tortured body, like I was just telling a wild story to the Situation after it was grown up.

At that point I was mostly crawling around on my hands and knees with Mikayla's no-longer-white nightgown rucked up around my waist and the flashlight clutched in a death grip in my numb left hand. My ass and thighs were glazed with mud and needles like I was a giant Hostess Sno Ball. I was trying to breathe deeply, but sounded more like a beater car that wouldn't start.

I'd collapse on one side every so often, either half-blacked out or losing the will to live or both, but then more pain would hit and jolt me back up to my knees again. I cried and screamed and swore and begged I don't even know who, but nobody came. I reached up to touch Wash's lucky cross, but it was gone.

I blacked out again, no idea how long, and was screaming before I fully woke back up. I felt like I urgently needed to shit out one of those submersible mines from World War II and everything else I had left in my body came out, but it just wouldn't pass.

Then, this terrible burning and a feeling of something huge and heavy pressing down and I realized it was happening. There was something the size of a softball squeezing out between my legs. A head. A person's head. Not some abstract Situation anymore, but a real living person who might not be living for very much longer if I didn't figure out how to make this work.

I was still on my hands and knees, pushing with everything I had left in me, but I realized that there was nobody there to catch that soft head and prevent it from dropping down into the bloody mud between my legs.

I had to find a way to change positions, to get myself turned over with my ass on the ground so that I could reach the baby when it came out. Or at the very least, it wouldn't have so far to fall.

What happened next felt like a series of flashes, half-remembered images or sensations that seemed disjointed and terrifying. This hot, slick weight passing through me and out of me so suddenly that it felt like being dismembered. This ragged, unnerving keening echoing in my raw throat, harmonizing strangely with sputtering gasps and cries coming from the mud between my legs. Fumbling with cold, slippery fingers to open a blade on the mini-Leatherman tool, presumably to cut the thick cord that was still hanging out of me, but I don't remember succeeding. I do remember how dirty the baby was, bits of leaves and needles clinging to this horrible whitish coating all over its shuddering body. Her body.

A girl.

A thick crop of wet black hair like some kind of pelt. So impossibly tiny and frail, like a runt rat pup that had been pushed out of the nest. Squashed red face and a baffled squint like she couldn't believe where she had ended up. I couldn't believe it either, to be honest. Because all this time I'd been refusing to think too hard about the Situation, it had been growing into this tiny girl human that was here now, alive against all odds with a lot to say about that.

I remember lifting her up out of the mud and trying to hold on to her, but my arms felt too weak. I remember her meager weight laying on my chest, her head under my chin, and the crying stopped. Was that because she was ok? Or was it because she wasn't?

I remember thinking I should do something about that piece of umbilical cord hanging out of me like a devil's tail. I pulled and twisted it, and then it came loose with this skinny purple rag attached and I thought maybe I'd torn off a piece of myself.

I must have blacked out then, because the next thing that I remembered was hot, meaty breath on my face and the sound of soft panting and a spike of adrenaline shot through me, wrenching me from lolling twilight consciousness and into cold, primal fear.

An animal. A wolf? Something was sniffing me. Something was sniffing the baby.

I shoved myself back and tried to partially sit up, holding tightly to the sticky, shivering baby, swinging the lipstick-sized blade on the Leatherman before I even realized I was doing it.

Illuminated by the weakening beam of the key-chain flashlight, the animal trotted away from me and my uncoordinated flailing, unfazed, and nonchalant, and that's when I realized it was wearing a brightly colored, handmade leather collar. It was a dog, a long-legged hound mix with crooked ears and chocolate-chip spots all over and a big, slobbery grin.

I heard a piercing whistle somewhere far away, and I must have passed back out again because the next thing I knew there were human hands on me.

I fought weakly, clinging to the impossibly small and fragile baby and making noises that were supposed to be the word no, but didn't really come out as anything even close.

"It's ok Angel," a familiar voice said. "It's ok."

Was that Chase? Or was I imagining it?

I wanted to tell whoever it was that of fucking course it wasn't ok, that it would never be ok again, but that narcotic blackness kept sucking me back under. Maybe there was somebody else there too, and it felt like I was being dragged and I lost track of the baby.

"Didi," I told somebody. "Her name is Didi. Tell her that's her name."

Then, nothing.

47.

When I came back to something like consciousness, I was indoors somewhere that smelled like woodsmoke and old books and mildewed plastic. I seemed to be lying on a heap of musty blankets on the floor. There was a cast iron stove near my head, but I was still ice cold. I couldn't stop shivering, and there was a fat, wet wad of something between my legs, like a bunched-up towel. More rags and towels were all around me, all different colors and all saturated with dark blood. I hurt all over, but especially down there.

There was a beautiful, older Native American woman sitting cross-legged on the floor to my left. She seemed like she was maybe in her early sixties, but had a round, smooth, almost childlike face under a felt hat with a feather in the band. A sturdy, solid build under a man's plaid work coat and she had this tangle of mismatched necklaces around her neck. Some seemed like cat toys or plastic junk jewelry like you'd give a kid to play dress-up and some seemed beautifully crafted with chunky stones and delicate silver. Some didn't seem like jewelry at all, more like pieces of colored string.

I grabbed her sleeve, or tried to but my fingers weren't a hundred percent on board with the idea.

"Why am I bleeding so much?" I asked. "Am I dying?"

She looked down at me, face serious and stoic for a long moment and then cracked a grin and let out a soft chuckle.

"How the fuck should I know?" she said. "I'm just here to buy grass."

This was not the midwife, obviously.

Whoever she was, she raised a freshly rolled joint to her wrinkled lips and lit it, took a deep, long pull off it and then held it out to me. I waved it away.

"Where's Didi?" I asked, suddenly lightheaded and dizzy.

"Chase?" the woman who wasn't Winnie called over her shoulder.

Chase appeared from behind the woman, and I saw that he was holding the baby cradled against his chest, feeding her with a glass bottle like he knew exactly what he was doing. The woman reached up and stuck the joint between Chase's lips. He sucked in smoke and then blew it away from the baby in a thick stream and that couldn't be a good idea, could it? But nothing I had done since the day I found out about the Situation that would become this hungry little person could be classified as a good idea, and even if I wanted to say something to him about it, I could feel myself graying out again.

When the world came back into focus, there was a man I didn't know trying to get me to drink water. My body wanted that water desperately, but my head felt too heavy to lift.

The man seemed to be in his late seventies or older, skinny as a Slim Jim with piercing dark eyes and a ratty, yellowish white beard that was nearly as long as his hair. Cheekbones that could cut glass and ears that seemed too big to be supported by his scrawny rooster neck. His hands looked like tree roots, but they were gentle on the back of my head as he lifted me to drink.

"Is..." I took a tiny swallow of water. "Is Winnie here?"

"She's right there," he said, gesturing to his left.

It seemed like a huge effort to turn my head, but I managed and saw my supposed savior sitting in a ratty armchair by a dark window on the other side of the stove. She was wearing an old Ramones t-shirt and an ankle-length cotton skirt that looked roughly handmade. Her gray hair was thickly dreadlocked and hung almost to the floor. She was maybe a little younger than him but just as skinny. The shirt hung like a sail on her flat chest and narrow, bony shoulders. Her feet were bare and dirty. Her mouth was slack, and her dark eyes were a million miles away.

"I'm afraid she's retired," the man who had to be Harlan said. "Guess you're stuck with me."

The whole fantasy of this idyllic mountain sanctuary where I would be safe and well cared for in a cute log cabin had never been real, but I'd still hung on to it anyway, and now I was here, in this grimy shack a thousand miles away from any kind of life I'd ever known.

"I'm Harlan," the man said. "Can't make Winnie's famous biscuits to save my life, but I helped her deliver one hundred and fifty-seven babies so I guess I may have learned a thing or two in that department."

I didn't want to ask him if I was going to be ok, because I dreaded the answer. Everything inside me felt jagged and wrong.

"Is Didi going to be ok?" I asked instead.

He smiled. Unlike his grandson, he'd somehow managed to keep all his stained and crooked teeth.

"She's tiny," he said. "But she's a warrior. Just like her mom."

I made a soft scoffing sound and took another drink.

"I'm a lover, not a fighter," I said.

"Well," he replied. "You better hang on to that love. Because you're gonna need it."

48.

I was bleeding to death. After all my years on camera, I didn't have much shame left about men looking at my body, but whatever dregs might have remained were long gone by then. It took more strength than I had to care about a man I barely knew and one I didn't know at all cleaning the endless mess between my legs. I felt weak and dizzy, but my heart was pounding, and I would constantly forget where I was. I kept thinking I was on set, that everyone was annoyed and waiting for me to get my shit together for the last scene of the day. I talked to Thick Vic, to Cody, to Hank. I tried to slap and punch at whoever kept on bothering me down there, but my hands were too heavy to lift.

"Shouldn't we try to get her to a hospital?" Chase was asking. "Maybe Nadine..."

"No," I said, squeezing somebody's hand now. Whose hand? "No fucking hospital."

"She wouldn't survive the trip," Harlan said. "She's either gonna make it here or she won't."

I must have blacked out again, but when I came to, the woman in the chair was no longer in the chair.

She was standing over me, silent, rheumy eyes locked on some unknowable horizon, but her hands moved with confident strength over the surface of my distended belly. She felt her way over the area just above my pelvic bone and then leaned her meager weight into me like I was a nearly empty tube of toothpaste, and she didn't want any of it to go to waste.

"What's she..." I thought I heard Chase say.

"Leave her," Harlan replied. "Her mind is gone, but her hands remember."

The woman kept on massaging and squeezing my tortured belly for what felt like forever but then there was a sudden feeling of weird pressure and then something passed out of my body, something that felt nauseatingly slick and fat, almost like giving birth to a second baby. Then another piece of something, this one even larger than the first and then a cascade of smaller pieces. The woman smiled and patted my belly like I had done a good job of whatever the hell just happened. I figured I should smile back or say something, but I was too busy passing back out.

I guess I didn't die, but I kind of wish I had.

49.

I'd been moved from my spot on the floor by the stove to a little alcove with a narrow bed and a threadbare curtain for an illusion of privacy in the tiny house. Harlan slept in a loft above me, accessible only by a rickety ladder, and Chase slept on a rough bedroll on the floor next to Didi's apple-box crib. Winnie slept, if you want to call it that, in her chair. The chocolate chip hound had taken my old spot by the stove. I had no idea how much time passed.

Chase had Didi wrapped up like a living burrito in a blanket made from faded bandanas stitched together with brightly colored thread and he was singing softly to her, some old murder ballad that sounded sweet but was probably not the best choice for little ears.

Little ears, Mikayla had said. Another dead person living inside my head forever, apparently. I was developing quite a collection.

"Go on to your mama, Mouse," he said, bending down over my bed to hand her to me.

My arms still felt dangerously weak, but I obligingly held them out to receive the baby burrito. It felt like an inert package against my chest.

I looked down at Didi's little face. She looked deeply skeptical, like Edward G. Robinson trying to figure out if you were trying to pull one over on him. Her brown eyes were just like mine.

I was waiting for something to happen, for the lovey-dovey bonding thing to kick in, when she suddenly started to cry.

"It's ok," I forced myself to say, thinking I should bounce her or rock her or something like people do with crying babies, but my arms felt dead and cold like I had forgotten what they were for. "It's ok."

She wasn't buying it. Her little body arched inside the burrito like she was getting shock treatment and the crying dialed up to full on screaming.

Holding the shrieking baby, I suddenly imagined myself flinging her away from me. Not just dropping her but actively throwing her as hard as I could against the wall. For a drowsy, terrible moment, it was as if that was really happening, and I was watching myself do it from outside my body. I watched as her soft pink face smashed first into the wall and then the floor. I saw her skinny little neck snap, blood on her dark hair just like mine used to be.

But it wasn't happening. What was happening was that my heart was skitter-pounding, breath suddenly ragged and blood roaring in my ears so loud that it almost seemed to drown out the crying. There wasn't enough oxygen in my little alcove, and I felt like I was suffocating and there was that fucking smell again, that chemical sting of burning duct tape choking me and I thought I was screaming too, but what came out was more like a sob.

"Take her," I said. "I can't. I can't."

Chase took Didi, who instantly settled down the second she was in his arms.

She hates me, I thought. *They all hate me.*

I pulled the curtain and turned my face to the wall.

50.

Not sure if it happened suddenly or if it had been slowly creeping up on me the whole time, but I realized sometime around the first snowfall that I was no longer connected to anything that was happening in the house. I felt like an untethered astronaut drifting through the killing cold of deep space just outside the steel hull of a busy space station. I could see in through the windows, I could see my fellow astronauts working and sleeping and laughing and going about their days in a perfectly normal way, but I couldn't seem to signal them to let them know how far away I had drifted.

I barely ate. I didn't bathe. I'd tell you that I mostly slept, but that's not entirely true. I mostly laid down with my eyes closed, trapped in a kind of sludgy, awful limbo between sleeping and waking.

I could see the baby, my baby, Didi, down there inside the cozy house but I couldn't connect to her in any way. I watched Chase blow raspberries on her belly while wrapping a cloth diaper around her scrawny, kicking legs and then put her to bed in her apple crate. I watched Harlan fashion a makeshift baby carrier out of an old canvas mail bag so Chase could tote her around outside while he fetched water and chopped wood. Sometimes he would put Didi in Winnie's arms for a few minutes, and the old woman would seem to come briefly back to life, cooing and smiling. But if I watched their activities for too long, I could see Didi's little face and fragile body shattered by bullets meant for me. I could see Chase dying face down in his own blood. I could see them all dead because of me, and I had to close my eyes again. To turn my face away from the warm glow of the windows and back towards the soul-killing emptiness between the stars.

"She's got the blues," Harlan said to Chase like I wasn't right there. Which wasn't entirely untrue, if I was honest. "That'll happen when a kid comes hard."

The Blues. It sounded so silly and inadequate to describe the way I felt. Like the fucking Blues Brothers were gonna show up and bust into a musical number. Like you're broke and your woman is running around. Not like this. Because there was feeling low down deep inside and there was *being* low down deep inside.

From that point on, Harlan started brewing these concoctions for me to drink, or drops to put on my tongue. CBD variations and herbs of one sort or another. The flavors ranged from graveyard dirt to moonshine brewed in a worn jockstrap to burnt lawn clippings. Each more awful than the last. Turned out he was a bit of a mad scientist about that kind of thing, and he seemed to be trying so hard that it was easier to just say that I was doing better, that it was working.

It was not working. I was not better.

51.

It was getting dark earlier and earlier until it seemed like there was hardly any daylight left at all. I was given work to do eventually, because even though I'd gotten a pass while I was recovering from the chainsaw massacre of Didi's birth, I learned pretty quick that everybody was expected to pull their own weight on the mountain. Everyone but Didi and Winnie.

Despite Wash's warning that Harlan was a mean old crank, he was surprisingly gentle as he doted on Winnie, feeding her mashed apples and honey and talking softly to her about old times. He read out loud to her from dusty novels packed into floor-to-ceiling shelving built into every wall like insulation against the creeping chill. She would sometimes wander off and come back all dirty and scraped up, and Chase would try to convince Harlan to figure out a way to restrain her for her own safety, but he would just shake his head with this little faraway smile.

"Can't hold down a wild-hearted woman that way," he said. "Wouldn't dream of it."

"But she could die out there," Chase replied.

"That's her choice," he said, washing her gently with a pan of rainwater heated on the stove. "When she's ready to go, she'll go."

I still couldn't do much, but I was tasked with scrubbing diapers and keeping the ancient cast-iron wood stove burning. I pretty much sleepwalked through the former but actually kind of enjoyed the latter.

At first I was nervous about anything to do with fire, still feeling the lingering trauma of everything that went down at the Hookin' B ranch and sure that I would make a terrible mistake that would either burn us alive or freeze us to death. But, even though Harlan was clearly used to doing everything by himself, he was actually a good teacher. He showed me how to rake and nurture the coal bed. How to bank the fire for the night and rekindle it in the morning. In a way, it felt like caring for a beautiful and dangerous pet. Funny how I felt utterly incapable of caring for Didi in even the most basic ways, but I somehow managed to keep that fire going. It gave a little structure to my dark, cold and endless days. It was certainly more fun than diaper duty.

The woman I met that first day turned out to be a neighbor named Nadine who would come by every so often with more formula and instant coffee and news from town. She brought beeswax and bullets. She brought hand-me-down baby clothes for Didi and a little hat she knitted out of this thick, pea-soup-colored wool that looked shorn from Oscar the Grouch. She brought books to swap with Harlan. She brought a guitar for Chase and I can't say for sure what he gave her in trade, but I have a pretty good idea. One time she brought a dead deer wrapped up in a tarp like a mafia murder victim and she and Chase butchered it right in the front yard, tossing occasional snacks to the drooling hound.

Mostly she came for marijuana from the three large, cylindrical greenhouses, and I got the feeling she was trading the stuff up and down the ridge on Harlan's behalf. Those greenhouses were the only modern structures on the property, with solar panels and automated irrigation and steady, gentle heating to keep the crops lush and verdant all year round. I had to carefully bank our wood stove by candlelight every night like some kind of fucking pioneer woman only one bad snowstorm away from cannibalism, but those pampered plants could relax all winter in their high-tech sauna. Nobody was allowed inside the greenhouses but Harlan.

Sometimes I thought about L.A. or tried to. All those fragmented images of leggy palm trees and sunglasses and video cameras all trained on me. Taco trucks and traffic on the 405 and the L.A. River, which was never really a real river, more like another empty, unfulfilled Hollywood dream. I had a life there once, but it was getting harder and harder to remember.

52.

Maybe I was getting better, or maybe just better at faking being better.

I still felt no emotional connection to Didi but I was able to hold her for several minutes and even give her a bottle once in a while without picturing myself throwing her to the ground. She accepted being held by me for short spells and would take food from any of us when she was hungry, but her eyes were always looking for Chase.

It's pretty ironic that I had plenty of free-flowing colostrum for all those pervs before Didi was born but now that she was here and hungry, my sad, empty tits had nothing left to offer. She didn't seem to care. She was perfectly happy sucking down formula cut with raw goat's milk, as long as Chase wasn't too far away.

"Put her up on your shoulder and rub her back," he said after her bottle was empty.

"How do you know so much about how to take care of a baby?" I asked, doing what he had suggested.

"Well you see," he replied, warming to the story as he stacked fresh firewood behind the stove. "My mama was a thoroughbred knockout. Legs for days, like she walked right out of a magazine, and she had a powerful thirst. Not just for liquor but for male attention. Daddy was off rodeoing most of the time and she got restless. It was like she didn't know who she was unless she had every dick in the room pointed in her direction."

I'd never drank, but it felt like a hundred years since I had a dick pointed in my direction and that felt painfully relatable. I certainly didn't know who I was anymore. I spent so many years seeing myself magnified through the lens of male desire that I never even imagined what life would be like after that desire dried up.

I wondered briefly if I would ever consider sex with Chase. I had always been a sucker for a charismatic fuckup, but I felt so disconnected from my body and the crime scene between my legs that I couldn't even stand the thought of it. Not just with him, but with anyone. It didn't help that the last dick that had been pointed at me was attached to a guy I killed.

If Chase noticed my inner turmoil, he didn't say anything. He just let the momentum of his storytelling carry him along while I rubbed and patted Didi's hot little back.

"So every time mama went looking to scratch that itch," he continued, "us kids had to figure things out for ourselves. My job was mostly to bullshit bill collectors and keep the landlord from knowing we was home alone, but there was always little ones needing something. Couldn't help but pick up the basics before I took off looking to scratch my own itch at age thirteen."

"You have kids of your own, right?"

"I got two boys." He looked away, suddenly taciturn. "Fifteen and thirteen. They call their stepfather Daddy. Don't want nothing to do with me."

I handed Didi back to him.

"Always wanted a little girl though," he said, more to her than me. He adjusted her pea-soup hat. "A pretty little baby girl."

Didi made a trilling sound as if to confirm that yes she was, in fact, pretty. I wondered if she would grow up with that same desire for male attention and how that might shape her life, but that thought was too big and slippery and I was feeling cold and exhausted and it was easier to let myself drift away into the bleak emptiness of my inner space.

*

Harlan was sitting on the edge of the bed in my alcove with food for me, some kind of smoky fish stew. I couldn't remember the last time that I had eaten.

"You're gonna need a new name," he told me. "A new first name for you and a last name for you and the baby."

"Not Washburn?" I asked, taking the bowl and spoon.

He made a soft chuffing noise under his beard.

"I'm flattered, of course," he said. "But no. You'd best distance yourself from any and all connections to the past." He leaned in closer to me. "And I'll let you in on a little secret. Washburn ain't my real name either. I got that name from a guitar that was left in my apartment in the Village by a girl singer I had a crush on about a hundred years ago. Got Harlan from the writer, Harlan Ellison."

"The Village?" I forced myself to eat a spoonful of the stew. It was actually not bad, but I still struggled to swallow. "You mean in New York City?"

"Born and raised," he said. "Got into all kinds of trouble fighting against the fascist pigs back in the day, so I wound up having to get lost. Which is how I wound up out here." He put out his hand like he was meeting me for the first time. "Julius Shulberg."

I switched the bowl to my left hand and took it.

"Gina Moretti," I said. It felt strange to say my real name out loud. "Better known as Angel Dare."

"Not anymore you ain't," he said.

Neither one of us said anything for a long minute. I put the stew down and pushed it away, unfinished.

"Well," I said. "I didn't have a pet growing up and we lived on 33rd street, plus I already have a porn name, so…"

"Why don't you pick something from the other end of the alphabet?"

I remembered this gorgeous French neighbor I had growing up named Zoe Vienne. She wore red lipstick and no bra and drove all the boys crazy. I thought she was so impossibly cool. I had considered using her name before I settled on Angel.

"Maybe I'll be Zoe."

"Zoe what?"

That was easy.

"Zoe Wyman."

"Zoe and Didi Wyman," he said. "Ok."

For a minute there, it almost seemed like there might be some kind of future.

53.

I started noticing the glint that spring.

At least it seemed like it might be spring. I had no real sense of time passing on the space station, but it seemed a little less frigid. There was a little less wood being gobbled up by the stove. Pointy green shoots were breaking through the dirty ice. It rained more than it snowed.

Didi was getting big, heavy and hardy and it was hard to believe that this was the same shivering rat baby that almost died with me that night out in the stoic, misty woods. Her big brown eyes were drinking in everything all around her all the time.

I noticed this fact like I noticed all those other things, but it didn't seem to have anything to do with me. She was Chase's baby now, always reaching her pink starfish hands to clutch at him, yanking at his beard and happily guzzling down a bottle that he'd fixed for her, cooing and gurgling while he sang to her like she was trying to harmonize with him. Miss Mousey, Chase called her, after her favorite song about a courting frog.

Chase was changing too. His doughy little beer-belly was gone. His body had been whittled down and streamlined and his face was leaner under the thick, luxurious beard and no-longer waxed mustache. No more dark, puffy circles under those clear gray eyes. He still availed himself of the bounty from Harlan's greenhouses, but I hadn't seen him take a drink since we got here. He had finally stopped running, and he was thriving on the mountain, while I was wasting away to nothing.

Didi and Chase were happy together. Happy without me. It was better that way.

I knew I had been backsliding into the cold, dark blues when Harlan started taking care of the stove again. He didn't say anything about it, just did it. I clearly couldn't be trusted to do anything but scrub shitty diapers and even that was oftentimes beyond me. I was useless, a liability. A drain on everyone around me.

When I wasn't trapped in that terrible limbo between sleeping and waking, I sometimes stood by the window on the other side of the stove, looking out at the melting world. There was this weird tree that had been split crookedly down the middle somehow and didn't die. Hit by lightning, maybe. Whatever it was, it was clearly a very long time ago. It stood watch over the outhouse, non-judgmental. That outhouse wasn't much to look at. It was small and crooked on one side and had been decorated with painted flowers and fantastical birds that had faded away to just the faintest suggestion of a petal here or a wing there. The view out the other window was nicer, the one where you could see the humpbacked greenhouses and the scrappy, playful goats and when it wasn't too foggy you could even see the creek and the swimming hole, cold shimmering water reflecting the soaring, saw-toothed mountain peaks behind it. But that window was on Winnie's side, so I always ended up looking out at the outhouse side. I did like that one tree, though.

I was looking at the tree when I saw the glint in the tangled brush behind the tree line. It was the first sunny day in ages and there was this tiny, fleeting flash, like the sunlight reflecting off somebody's glasses as they turned their head.

Or the reflection off of a gun sight.

My heart kicked in my chest, and I felt this sudden dizzying rush of panic as I clutched at the windowsill.

"Did you…?" I said, trailing off before I could finish with *see that*.

Chase and Harlan had gone off somewhere together with Didi

in her mailbag and it was just me and Winnie in the cabin. How long had they been gone?

I looked back out the window, but I didn't see the glint again until the next morning.

Soon I was spending the majority of my time at that window. I would scan that area behind the outhouse over and over again, stomach in knots and body turned sideways to hide behind the rumpled curtain. Because if someone was there, I needed to know so that I could warn Chase. I didn't want to say anything too soon, because what if I was wrong?

But what if I wasn't?

I had been sleeping way too much, but suddenly sleep was impossible. I was up all hours of the night, checking that window, scanning the darkness, heart struggling like a snared and panicked animal inside my aching chest, choking on the smell of burning duct tape.

We would all die if I didn't check. The one time I was too tired to check, it would be all over and it would be my fault, just like every other bad thing that ever happened to anyone who knew me.

I couldn't make myself go outside at all anymore. If I got anywhere even near the door, I was hit with intense, full-body anxiety bordering on terror. I reverted to using the chamber pot under my bed.

I would just stand for hours by the window staring into the tree line, listening to the wind rustling in the pine branches and was that a human voice under the crackle of a staticky police radio or did I imagine it?

Nadine came by one morning while I was staring out the open window at the rustling tree line. It had been several weeks since I'd seen her last, and this time she didn't bring anything to trade. Harlan was coming out of one of the greenhouses and she quickly intercepted him, pulling him close and turning away from the house. She was speaking softly, but I caught fleeting fragments of what she was telling him.

"...asking around..."

"...be careful..."

Then I swear I thought I heard her say something that froze my blood.

Corbin.

But she couldn't have said that, could she? How would she know anything about Corbin?

Again, that staticky sound like a distant police scanner and the voice on the radio seemed to echo the name again and again.

Corbin. Corbin. Corbin.

For several minutes, I was trapped in the kind of thick, sludgy dread that you feel when you have those nightmares where you're trying to run away in slow motion but the monster is gaining on you. I couldn't move. Couldn't speak. I wanted to race outside, grab Nadine by the shoulders and shake her and make her tell me everything. But it was like I was already a ghost, invisible to the living and unable to communicate. Like I was trapped in the moment right before my own brutal murder forever.

There was a tiny, deeply buried part of me that knew I wasn't thinking right. That I wasn't really hearing secret messages on a police scanner. That Nadine could have been talking about anything, that I could have misheard her. That the glint could have been anything, or nothing at all. That it wasn't the end of the world and nobody was going to die.

But sometimes that part of me was silent.

54.

Look, I've been telling you everything that happened in as honest and unflinching a way as I know how. I've tried not to shy away from the gory details or try to make myself look any better or more heroic than I really am. I haven't held anything back, but nothing I've told you so far was harder for me to admit than what I'm about to tell you.

It was dawn. A cold, silvery fog clung to the surface of the swimming hole and hung in tatters from the swaying branches of pine trees. I'd had another long, terrifying night at the window, but I wasn't entirely sure how I got outside in the first place, let alone how I wound up standing in the water.

The water was so cold it burned as it lapped up against my knees. I couldn't feel my feet. Did I have shoes on? I could hear Didi crying, but it seemed so far away, and I wasn't that worried about it anyway because it wouldn't be going on for much longer.

I remember thinking, *This is it. For real this time. Just a few more steps, and it will finally be over.*

I took one step, then another. The water was up to my crotch now. It seemed like the cold should have been worse, but I was already so frozen that it didn't seem to make that much of a difference. The crying got louder but so did the voices on the police scanner. I had to hurry, before they found us. This was the only way.

I'd been so weak. So utterly chickenshit, so deep in denial about how bad things could get. So stupid and helpless and such a crushing burden on everyone around me. A killing burden. I was a lightning rod for death and destruction, and I needed to break out of this poisonous inertia and take decisive action. To do something to stop this madness. I just needed to take another step.

But somehow, that next step felt like the hardest. Like the step off the edge of a skyscraper. The water was up to my waist now, but I still had at least two or three more steps to go before my head would be under. So why was this step so hard?

You know why, don't you?

It was because I was holding the baby.

"I'm sorry, Didi," I said, but I wasn't sure if I was talking to the baby or to my old friend. My old dead friend. Did it really matter anyway?

All those times when I'd wanted to off myself but didn't because I was pregnant, I'd been so wrong. It would have been so much easier back then, before I could hear her crying. But in that moment, there was no doubt in my mind that killing us both was the only way to prevent the inevitable bloody massacre that played out on the drive-in movie screens of my eyelids every time I closed my eyes. There was no scenario in which Zoe and Didi Wyman lived happily ever after. I'd let myself be passive far too long, and now it was time to take action before somebody else did it for me. At least this way, it would be over quickly.

I slid my right foot forward on the slimy creek bed, about to take that next step, when I noticed I wasn't alone in the water.

I hadn't heard her get in, but there she was as if she had manifested suddenly out of the morning fog like some kind of pale apparition. Winnie, standing in the water to my left in her wet flannel nightgown. She didn't speak or even look at me. She just stood there and then slowly, moving like a plant turning towards the sun, she put her hand gently on my shoulder. Not clutching at me or trying to pull me back, just resting there.

We stood like that for ages. Nothing happened. The baby cried and squirmed. I was starting to shiver. It was now or never. I slid my foot forward in preparation to take one more step, but didn't. I couldn't.

Winnie moved her hand down my arm, turning her body towards me and slipping her cold fingers under Didi's arched and trembling back.

I let her take the baby. I couldn't do anything right. Not even this.

Pathetic.

Now that Didi's weight was gone from my arms, it was replaced by an immense and suffocating shame. My whole body felt like it was about to collapse, to break into a million frozen shards. I don't know if I was intending to throw myself into the deep water at that point or if I just lost my footing because my legs gave out, but I was staggering, twisting, falling away from Didi. Away from hope. Away from everything.

That's when I got shot.

Anyone out there who's looking for a cure for postpartum depression ought to try getting shot. Nothing like a surge of life-or-death adrenaline to snap you out of a suicidal black hole.

Pain radiated through my left shoulder and arm, hot blood running down my icy back, but I somehow still wasn't dead. Despite my best intentions.

Then I heard more shots coming from the opposite direction, and Chase was suddenly splashing into the water. He threw an arm around me and the other around Winnie and Didi, pushing us down and towards the shore. Harlan provided a cover of gunfire aimed at the tree line.

More shots came our way as well, most of them striking the

surface of the water behind us with a sound like hail. But one—one plowed into Winnie from behind and she fell forward, pulling Chase's arm down as she collapsed to her knees in the shallows.

Someone *had* been watching us. Someone was here to kill us all.

Just because you're paranoid, doesn't mean they aren't out to get you.

55.

Chase took Didi from Winnie's arms as she stumbled. Winnie didn't scream or cry. She just turned to me looking slightly puzzled like a person trying to remember the name of a song.

Harlan called her name, but she didn't respond. Didi was screaming, screaming so loud I couldn't hear anything else and was that my blood on her little face or was she hit too?

The pain in my shoulder was burning like wildfire, racing down my back and up the side of my neck but I still felt so cold. I didn't feel like I could trust my body to do anything it was told. My legs felt like they weighed five hundred pounds each.

Things got a little sketchy then. I saw Harlan with his rifle slung back over his shoulder, pulling Winnie's limp, wet body towards the shore with her steel-gray dreads trailing like tentacles across the surface of the bloody water. Chase had zipped Didi up inside his jacket with only her head sticking out and was shooting back at the tree line with a pistol, his hand covering one of her little ears and pressing the other against his chest. She was screaming and I wanted to join her, but didn't.

Nadine's truck came flying up the muddy drive, her steering with one hand and shooting out the rolled-down window with the other. One of the goats got hit by a stray bullet at some point and the others bucked and bleated in terror, throwing themselves against the confines of their pen. I have no idea what happened to the dog, but I like to believe he got spooked and ran away to hide. Not much of a guard dog, apparently.

I saw Chase duck behind one of the greenhouses and I tried to follow but was cut off by a spray of bullets throwing up dirt and moss and chips of stone. I hit the ground with a stifled grunt of pain and crawled around the side of the chicken coop, enveloped in the harsh, metallic stench and dust and drifting feathers. It should have felt silly to be trying to avoid dying when less than a minute before I had been trying for the opposite effect, only my body had automatically defaulted to hindbrain-level, second-by-second survival mode.

Or at least that's what I thought at first. But something else was happening too, something I couldn't quite put my finger on. I'd felt like a threadbare ghost, just going through the motions and disconnected from everything for so long that I forgot what it felt like to be alive and present in the moment. Everything felt crisp and sharp and vivid now. Guns and blood and a violent vendetta with innocent lives at stake and I knew what to do.

I felt like myself again.

"Where the fuck is the shooter?" Nadine was yelling as she dove out of her still-running truck to hunker down beside Harlan and Winnie's body.

"Your ten o clock," Chase yelled back. "But he's on the move!"

I had no idea where that would be but she clearly did because she drew a calm, steady bead on the patch of tree line where I first saw the glint.

I wish that I could say I felt vindicated that at least some of my hallucinations had been proven real, but I was too busy focusing on using the cover of Nadine's fire to make a run for that greenhouse.

I found Chase crouching beside a shot water pipe that was gushing like a slashed artery. Didi was still shrieking at the top of her little lungs, bright red and quivering with rage. A tiny warrior, Harlan had said. Just a few minutes ago, I had been so lost and broken that I was ready to take her down with me, but now I could see clearly that she was the only thing that mattered. That she and Chase had to be protected at all costs.

"You need to get Didi to the truck," I said. "Get her the hell out of here."

Chase nodded, slapped his gun into my open hand and cupped the back of Didi's head. I pointed the gun in the same direction as Nadine and fired off two shots while he hunched down, curled his whole body around Didi and ran for the passenger side of the truck.

I was scanning the tree line for that glint, trying to home in on any hint of the shooter when Nadine took one in the chest, blood blooming through her rough plaid coat as her wild and final shot was lost in the silvery gray sky.

Corbin stepped out of the tree line like the Grim fucking Reaper.

56.

He moved like a camo-clad automaton, taking smooth, measured steps across the yard. Like a school shooter caught on surveillance video, only this was happening to me. To us.

He wouldn't kill an innocent baby, would he?

Would he?

Chase had opened the passenger door of the truck and was using it for a shield while he unzipped Didi and shoved her to relative safety in the middle of the bench seat. He was reaching for an additional gun in Nadine's glove box when Corbin shot him in the ankle.

Chase dropped, screaming through clenched teeth, and tried to crab-crawl backward down the length of the truck, away from Didi. He never did manage to get that gun. Unarmed, he somehow got his good leg under him and launched himself at Corbin with everything he had. It wasn't anywhere near enough, and Corbin easily sidestepped him like he was avoiding a hug from an unpleasant drunk. Chase crumpled as Corbin raised the barrel of his rifle again.

He had Chase in his crosshairs, nearly point-blank. It would have been impossible to miss.

"Hey!" I yelled, waving my arms and lunging out from behind the greenhouse, away from Chase and back towards the swimming hole while keeping my body turned towards Corbin the whole time. In my mind I could hear the echo of Wash yelling *heyheyhey* in the arena back in Ada, drawing the bull away from the injured cowboy. "Over here, Corbin! *Here!*"

I drew Corbin's killing focus from Chase, calling it back to myself. Where it belonged.

"I'm the one you want," I said.

When I locked eyes with Corbin, my own avenging angel, I saw my own anguish in his eyes. I saw myself in him, eaten up inside with grief and rage and only surviving by promising to get me every single day. And now here we were together, finally, like me and Vukasin should have been. I had been wrong to try to off myself. There had never been any other end to this story. There was just me and him.

He pulled the trigger.

My heart was beating louder than bullets, pumping all the blood out of my body and into the cold mud between us. I thought I heard Harlan's voice somewhere far away, yelling for Chase to get in, and the sound of the truck engine gunning. I thought I heard tires crunching on the rocky dirt drive, driving away. I hope that's what I heard.

Dying means that you don't get to find out what happens next.

I was ok with that.

ACKNOWLEDGMENTS

Thanks to all the bullfighters, barrel men, stock contractors and other rodeo cowboys and girls who opened their lives, homes and hearts to this nosy New Yorker over the course of my research and travels. Evan Allard, Frank Newsom, Nate and Bridget Jestes, Logan and Kaley Mae Blasdell, Weston Rutkowski, Chuck Swisher, Cody Casto, Wacey Munsell, Dusty Tuckness, Cody Webster, Daryl Thiessen, Judd Napier, Zach Arthur, Zach Flatt, Andy North, Andy Burelle, Robbie Hodges, Lance Britton, Justin Josey, Hollywood Yates, Tanner Zarnetski, Kyle Lippencott, Erick Schwindt, Lelo Garcia, Nathan Harp, Chad Dowdy, Troy Lerwill, Jace Dunn, Rob Smets, Jim Hill, George Doak, Wayne Cornish, Randy Quartieri, Dale Brisby, Sammy Catalena and the Catalena Cowgirls, and all the crazy kids with BFO.

It's been ten long years and I'm sure I'm missing the names of a bunch more big-hearted and amazing people, so here's an extra shout-out to every single one of you. Please know that any and all fuck ups and/or wild deviations from the cold hard facts are 100% on me.

A big cowboy hat tip to my posse of beta readers, Heather Levy, Johnny Shaw, Jedidiah Ayers, Rob Hart and Nathan "Action" Long, and also to Dr. Jeff Paasch, DVM and post-partum doula Meredith Swierczynski for their insights into bovine and human reproduction.

Once again, thanks to my ride-or-die editor Charles Ardai, my agent Al Guthrie, and also to cover artist Paul Mann for picking up where the late, great Glen Orbik left off.

All this would be impossible without CDV, the Lady V and the late, great Mr. Tom.

Finally, I have to thank Nadine "Bull Heist" Nettmann for keeping the gag alive for way too long and Old Five and Dimer Ben Whitmer, who started me down this fucked-up rodeo trail in the first place.

Want to Know Where
Angel's Story Began...?

The Saga Begins in

MONEY SHOT

and Continues in

CHOKE HOLD

1.

Coming back from the dead isn't as easy as they make it seem in the movies. In real life it takes forever to do little things like pry open your eyes. You spend excruciating ages trying to bend your left middle finger down far enough to feel the rope around your wrists. Even longer figuring out that the cold hard thing poking you in the cheek is one of the handles of a pair of jumper cables. This is not the kind of action that makes for gripping cinema. Plus there are these long dull stretches where people in the audience would probably go take a piss or get popcorn, since it looks as if nothing is happening and they figure maybe you really are dead after all. After a while, you start to wonder the same thing yourself. You also wonder what will happen if you throw up behind the oily rag duct-taped into your mouth or how long it will take for someone to notice you're missing. Otherwise you are mostly busy bleeding, trying not to pass back out, or laboriously adding up the cables, the stuffy cramped darkness, the scratchy carpet below and the raw hollow metal above to equal your current location, the trunk of an old and badly maintained car. That's what it was like for me, anyway.

I'm sure you're wondering what a nice girl like me was doing left for dead in the trunk of a piece of shit Honda Civic out in the industrial wasteland east of downtown Los Angeles. Or maybe we've met before and you're wondering why it hadn't happened sooner.

My name's Gina Moretti, but you probably know me as Angel Dare. Don't worry, I won't tell your wife. I made my first adult video when I was twenty, though I lied on camera and said I was eighteen. It was volume one of Marco Pole's now-famous amateur line, *Brand Spankin' New*. My scene was just one of five but there's no question that I stole the show. What can I say? I know where my strengths lie. I had a contract with Vixen Video less than two weeks later and before I knew it I was on the Playboy Channel doing soft-focus video centerfold segments for more money than I earned in a year back home. A porno Cinderella story, but unlike so many of the girls I worked with, I was smart enough to stay off drugs, save every penny, and get out before my pussy turned back into a pumpkin.

Problem was, I just couldn't stay retired. Like a pro wrestler or a jewel thief, I was a sucker for an encore. I had no idea when I said yes to Sam Hammer that I'd end up stuffed in a trunk.

Sam's an old friend. One of the few genuine good guys left in the biz. Kind of a cross between Santa Claus and John Holmes. He must have been pushing sixty, burly and cheerful with a silver ponytail and neatly groomed beard. He was the kind of guy that always had a sofa to crash on or a shoulder to cry on, a loan till your next check or a guy he knew who would fix your toilet for cheap. I'd say he was like a father to me, but that would sound kind of weird since we did a few scenes together, back before he started working exclusively behind the camera. Never mind how long ago. He had been a perfect gentleman too, easygoing, respectful and reliable as clockwork. No easy feat before Viagra became the backbone of the industry, so to speak. Back when you actually had to count on feminine wiles to make the trains run on time, a man like Sam who could stand and deliver on cue was worth his weight in gold. Now you have guys popping Viagra and Cialis like Tic Tacs and shooting Caverject directly into the equipment to get things up and running. Better loving through chemistry.

Sam Hammer shoots were always a blast. No pressure. Sam was married to all-natural triple-D legend Busti Keaton, star of the *Topsy Turvy* series and *Battlestar Gazongas*. She would cook huge amounts of the best down-home comfort food and fuss around the set making sure nobody was too hot or too cold or uncomfortable in any way. I've been on plenty of jobs that were just jobs, or worse. Hammer shoots never felt like work. More like big happy Sunday barbeques where they just happened to be filming people having sex.

Sam could have easily made the jump to Hollywood. He had a great eye for composition and wrote witty, original scripts that actually kept your finger off the fast-forward button. But we all knew that he would never leave the Valley. Sam was a lifer. He liked being around naked girls way too much to go legit. So many smut directors are nothing but jaded hacks who spend most of the shoot snorting lines or talking on their cell phones, but not Sam. His enthusiasm was infectious.

When he called, I was having one of those days. Those sneaking-up-on-forty days when I can't stop looking in the mirror. Comparing what I see now to the image of that perfect, flawless little twenty year old bouncing around on top of Marco Pole for digital eternity. I'm in better shape now than I ever was, working out six days a week and kickboxing to knock out stress, but all the crunches in the world can't reverse gravity, or crow's feet, or the fact that I have to use the hair dye that advertises "100% gray coverage!" Don't get me wrong, I've got a pretty iron-clad ego, but I run Daring Angels, a high-class adult modeling agency out in Van Nuys, and being around all those gorgeous nineteen-year-olds sometimes gets to me. Makes a girl feel like yesterday's news.

When Sam called, I was standing in the full-length mirror beside my desk, topless and sideways. I have always been proud of the fact that I never had my tits done. I've seen way too many beautiful women ruined by ghastly, wall-eyed Frankenstein implants. Yet, on that day, I was hefting my assets in the palms of my hands and wondering if maybe they could use a little surgical pick-me-up after all.

I called my receptionist, personal assistant and all-around Mom Friday into my office. Didi was big back in the *Deep Throat* days, though if you saw her now, you'd never know it. She was fifty-two, five feet even, with a plain, sweet face like your favorite teacher, but underneath that G-rated exterior was an old-school porn veteran who talked about sex like other people talk about the weather. She had a rich, phone-sex purr of a voice and she got asked out on dates nearly every day by the men who called to book girls. More than half of the time she said yes, and though they may have done a double take when she showed up, I doubt any of those guys were sorry by the end of the night. Didi was probably the best thing that ever happened to me. I don't even want to think about how I would have run Daring Angels without her.

She came in the door with her sparkly vinyl purse on one arm and the other arm sliding into the sleeve of her pink leather jacket.

"What's up, boss?" she said. "I'm just out the door. Got a hot one lined up tonight." She looked down at my exposed breasts and rolled her eyes. "Would you stop it already! You do *not* need a goddamn boob job."

I grinned. "Go on, Didi. I'll see you tomorrow."

She blew me a kiss and split. I turned back to the mirror. I knew she was right, but still…

When I heard my phone's electronic chirp, I jumped a little, feeling like I'd been busted somehow.

"Daring Angels," I said.

"Angel, baby." Just hearing Sam's familiar growl was enough to cheer me up. "How you doing, beautiful?"

"Never better," I replied, turning away from the mirror and grabbing my push-up bra off the back of my chair. "You?"

"The usual," he said. "You know. Making dirty movies."

"How's Georgie?" I asked, holding the phone between my cheek and shoulder and hooking the bra around my ribs.

Georgie was Busti Keaton's real name. I should have noticed the tight little pause and the pinched tension in his voice as he answered much too quickly.

"Fine, she's real good. Listen, Angel, I got a favor to ask."

"Anything, Sam," I said, turning the bra around and slipping my arms through the straps, settling everything into place. I eyed my reflection. Much better.

"I'm shooting with Jesse Black," Sam told me. "I had a new girl flake on me and we've only got the location for another two hours."

I nodded and leaned over my laptop, calling up my booking calendar.

"Okay," I said scanning the schedule. "Zandora Dior and Kyrie Li are both out of town featuring, but Sirena, Coco Latte and Roxette DuMonde are available, or I've got this new kid, Molly May. She's a knockout, a legit redhead—carpet matches the drapes. Fresh, petite girl-next-door type but she also glamours up real nice. She's only a B-cup, though. It's not a busty line, is it? Bethany Sweet is my only current double-D and she's booked today."

"Actually," Sam said. "Jesse asked for you."

"Come on," I said, laughing nervously and turning back toward the treacherous mirror. "Sam, you know I'm retired."

"Angel, please, I really need your help on this. Jesse is threatening to walk out on me and I promised him I'd get him any girl he wanted. He wants Angel Dare. He says he cut his teeth on your movies, that you were his favorite since he was fifteen."

Now you have to realize that Jesse Black was probably the hottest new male talent in the biz. He was twenty-one, Hollywood handsome and legendary below the belt. The bluest blue eyes. Bad boy smile. More than half the women who'd come to me looking for work in the past six months said they got into porn specifically because they wanted to work with Jesse Black. Now Jesse Black wanted to work with me.

"It's pretty short notice, Sam," I said, already finding my mind shamelessly wandering over the details of Jesse Black's famous anatomy.

"No anal," Sam replied. "Just a simple little boy/girl scene with a facial pop. I can give you fifteen and a cover. It'll be like old times."

I had to admit it was appealing. It'd be a phone-in, plus Jesse Black, plus helping Sam, plus an easy fifteen hundred bucks and a big fat box cover ego boost. Proof I've still got it. I could feel my resistance wearing down fast, but I had to keep trying.

"I don't have a current test," I said. "It's been almost seven months."

"You can just fax it in to me by Monday," Sam said. "Look, I'll make it two grand."

"Sam...I..."

"Okay, twenty five, what do you say? I'm in a jam here, Angel. My last three videos tanked and if I screw this one up too, I'll probably get shitcanned from Blue Moon. But with Angel Dare and Jesse Black on the box cover, I got a sure thing."

He was starting to sound desperate. If it had been anyone else, I probably would have held my ground, but Sam had always been there for me whenever I needed anything. No questions asked.

"Okay, Sam," I said. "Jesse knows I'm condom only?"

"Sure," Sam said. "It's no problem. Look, I'll put him on, okay?"

"Wait," I said but it was too late.

"Angel?" a new voice said. "Is this Angel Dare?"

"In the flesh," I said. "This Jesse?"

"Yeah," he replied. "Angel Dare, wow. I can't believe it's really you."

"It's me alright," I said, having no idea what else to say.

"God, you're so hot," he said. "I swear I must've worn out, like, three copies of *Double Dare*. That scene you did with Nina Lynn in the shower." He made a breathy little purring noise. "Damn."

"Thanks," I said, eyeing my reflection again. Back when I shot *Double Dare*, Jesse probably still thought girls were icky. It seemed so wild that a toddler like him would have the hots for me. "You're not so bad yourself, kid."

"Will you do it?" he asked. "Please say you'll do it. It'll be like my best fantasy come true. Me and Angel Dare."

"Well..." I said.

"I'll make it good for you, Angel," he said, voice raw and earnest, like my first boyfriend. "I promise."

"Put Sam back on, okay?" I said.

There was some quick shuffling and then Sam's voice came back on the line.

"Come on, Angel," Sam said. "Make the kid's day. He's gonna start humping me if you don't get here soon."

I sighed and grabbed a pen.

"What's the address?"

2.

The location was one of those sad old mansions in Bel Air. Ostentatious, but had seen better days. Money is so fickle here in L.A. and a big old house is like an aging mistress with a plastic surgery fetish. It's more economical to just buy a cheap, flashy new one than keep on renovating the old one. Otherwise, you wind up renting the place out for porn shoots just to break even on the roofing bills.

There was a pair of twisted pomegranate trees guarding the open gate and the ground beneath them was gory with broken crimson fruit that crunched and splattered under the wheels of my little black Mini. Pulling into the wide circular driveway, I kept expecting to spot Norma Desmond burying her pet chimpanzee in the overgrown rose garden. I felt better once I saw Sam's red '84 Corvette with its vanity plates that read HAMRXXX. It was parked near a massive wooden door that looked like it ought to open into a medieval Spanish dungeon. I parked behind Sam and got my old shoot bag off the passenger seat. There were a few other cars I didn't recognize in front of Sam's, a generic mid-sized rental and a tricked out, over-the-top black Ferrari that had to be Jesse's. Car like that just screamed dick-for-hire. Parked directly in front of the Ferrari was the battered blue Honda Civic with which I would soon become so intimately familiar.

I've spent a lot of time since then going over and over those short minutes in the driveway, wondering why I didn't sense something wrong, why I just waltzed right in like some barely legal bimbo from Indiana. I try to tell myself it was because I trusted Sam, because he was my friend for nearly twenty years, but if I'm honest I have to admit that was only part of it. The simple truth is, I had a girl boner. All the blood had run out of my brain and down between my legs. I'd had this semi-regular thing with a rockabilly bass player that had lasted nearly six months, but it had recently gotten stale and predictable and I'd decided it was time to move on. It had been three weeks since I'd gotten any new action. Now I found myself in a ditzy hormonal fog, gone blonde at the thought of putting Jesse Black's lean, hard, twenty-one-year-old body through its paces. So I walked, crotch-first, right into a trap.

The wheels of my little roller suitcase bumped along over the cracked pavement and the lonely echoing sound seemed way too loud in the deserted courtyard. The door wasn't locked. I thought they might be shooting some dialog or pick-up footage so I didn't knock. I just slipped quietly inside.

The first thing I noticed was that there was no furniture. It was a huge, hollow room with a cathedral ceiling, Spanish tile floors and a massive iron chandelier on a chain that looked like something Zorro would use to swing over the heads of the bad guys. There were several large windows, but they were covered with opaque plastic, letting in only a soft, muted fraction of the afternoon sun. It smelled like fresh paint.

"Angel?" Sam's voice called from the top of an elegant, curving staircase. "That you?"

"Yeah," I replied, squinting up the stairs.

"We're up here," Sam said.

I pushed down the telescoping handle on my case and hefted it to carry it up the stairs. Luckily, it was just the small shoot bag and nearly empty. Sam said I'd only need lingerie and heels so I had run by the house on my way over and thrown together a couple of sets and stockings to give him some options. It's been years since I had my shoot bags packed and ready all the time, everything organized into neatly labeled Ziploc bags and categorized with titles like *fetish*, *slut*, or *GND*, which stood for Girl Next Door.

"Sam?" I called when I got to the top of the steps.

"Come on in." Sam's voice came from the far end of a long hallway.

There was a partially open door with a bright light inside and I walked toward it. There were no fat yellow cords duct-taped to the floor, no adjacent rooms full of giggling girls powdering their implant scars and gluing on false eyelashes. There was no one hanging around smoking or talking on a cell phone. Just that long empty hallway. I like to think I was starting to wonder a little at that point, but I didn't leave. I just pushed the door the rest of the way open and went right in.

The room at the end of the hall was mostly empty, except for a large wrought-iron bed with a bare mattress covered in plastic. Sam stood against the far wall, beside an empty fire-place. There were two other men I didn't recognize, but I didn't get much of a look at them because Jesse was right by the door looking delicious, dark hair tousled and blue eyes smoldering, ready to go. He wore leather pants that hung so low on his lean hips that you would have seen his pubic hair if he hadn't shaved it off. His sleek, lanky torso was bare and sheened with sweat that highlighted the symmetrical perfection of every muscle. He stepped up to me, gave me an appreciative once-over and smiled.

"Angel Dare," he said. "Wow. You look amazing. This is gonna be awesome."

He reached down and squeezed his most famous feature through his tight leather pants. Then he punched me in the face.

The Assignment

by WALTER HILL

Kidnapped and operated on by the vengeful sister of one of his victims, a professional killer emerges permanently altered—and with a thirst for revenge of his own. Inspired the movie starring Michelle Rodriguez and Sigourney Weaver.

The Girl with the Dragon Tattoo

by STIEG LARSSON & SYLVAIN RUNBERG

The entire saga of Lisbeth Salander, adapted in three graphic novels—plus a fourth volume, *The Girl Who Danced With Death*, telling an all-new story unavailable in any other format.

Gun Honey

by CHARLES ARDAI

Joanna Tan will get you the weapon you need when you need it, no matter how impossible. But a government agency has her in its sights for a job with echoes from her bloody past.

Ryuko, Vol. 1 & 2

by ELDO YOSHIMIZU

From acclaimed international artist Yoshimizu, the bloody story of a daughter of the Yakuza and her quest to learn her mother's fate and redeem her suffering.